I0586045

BAIT

DARK MASQUE BOOK 1

MAGGIE ALABASTER

JO BRADLEY

Copyright © 2023 by Mirren Hogan writing as Maggie Alabaster and Jo Bradley

All rights reserved.

No part of this book may be reproduced in any form or by any electronic or mechanical means, including information storage and retrieval systems, without written permission from the author, except for the use of brief quotations in a book review.

Cover by Moonstruck Cover Design and Photography

Edited by Lily Luchesi

Proofread by Nora Hogan

CHAPTER ONE

KENNEDY

Whoever she was, she came so loudly she wouldn't have heard me sidestep them in the dark.

Apparently, I wasn't the only one sneaking away from the masquerade ball to get some air. Although, judging from the noise, she was getting a fuck load more than air.

"Oh yeah, baby, just like that," a male voice groaned.

I wrinkled my nose and hurried on through the trees. They probably didn't hear the twig snap under my foot, or the music that poured out of the ballroom and into the night. They wouldn't have heard anything but the roar of blood through their veins, and their moans.

I slanted away from them and headed toward the lake.

I pushed my mask off my face and up onto the top of my head. Strands of hair fell around my face, knocked loose by the elastic on either side of the mask. I pulled the clip out and let the rest of my red hair fall down my back, wild and wavy.

I picked up my skirt and stepped carefully over a fallen log. My black chiffon gown was long enough no one noticed I wore flat shoes instead of the heels my mother wanted. In sequin stilettos, I would have fallen flat on my face.

No thank you.

She also wanted me to wear pink, like I was still a kid or something. Pink would have clashed with my hair like bubblegum on a tomato. Thank fuck she listened to reason in the end. Although, only because she was busy with plans for her wedding. Fighting with me took a back seat for a change.

"I was on my way."

I froze at the sound of voices up ahead. How many couples had crept away for air?

I cocked my head and listened. The sound which carried on the breeze wasn't fucking. It was talking. Several voices. Tense, tight.

My breath held, I stepped toward them on silent feet.

"I tried to leave, but the boss, he needed..." The tremble of fear in the speaker's voice sent a shiver up my spine.

I stopped. I shouldn't be here, listening. Whatever was going on, they were out here in the night for a reason. Obviously. People didn't sneak around in the dark just for the hell of it.

"That's crap and you know it," another voice said. Also male. "We've given you enough chances. How many is it now?"

A third voice spoke but I couldn't make out the words.

"Please..." That was the first man. His words were accompanied by the sudden tang of urine. "I was an accident, I swear."

"Bullshit," the second guy growled.

Another shiver passed down my spine. I should leave, right now. Run. Or better yet, sneak away before they knew I was there.

Instead, I took a few more steps forward. A skewer of light from the ballroom faintly illuminated four figures. Two stood facing a third. He was restrained by the fourth, his arms held behind his back. They all wore dark suits. Masks, like the one I wore on top of my head, covered three of their faces. Only the restrained man had a bare face. No one I recognised, although I only arrived in Dusk Bay a week ago.

One of the masked men nodded to another. He drew something out of his pocket. A faint click and the light reflected off a slim blade in his hand.

Shit.

"Can we have some fun first?" the guy beside him asked. He cocked his head and smiled. "I bet he screams really pretty."

The restrained man sobbed. "Please... I swear I won't—"

Whatever he was going to say was cut off by the slice of the knife across his throat. He let out a gurgle. Light reflected off a gush of blood which poured from his open neck. His eyes bugged out of his face and he sagged.

I clapped a hand over my mouth. They just... Murdered the guy.

I hoped to hell they couldn't hear my heart racing. In my ears, it sounded louder than a passenger plane engine. Multiple rapid cracks of thunder.

My stomach turned. I wished I hadn't eaten my last several meals. They all threatened to make a violent reappearance on the ground at my feet.

I swallowed hard and forced several breaths in and out, silent and shallow.

I had a sneaking suspicion these guys wouldn't leave any witnesses alive. I had to calm down, not panic and do something stupid.

I crouched, shrunk as low as I could and held my breath.

"That was anticlimactic," the guy without the knife said. He snatched the blade and shoved it into the victim's eye. He pushed it in deeper, twisting it.

A short cry was cut off as the knife entered the man's brain.

Fucking hell. My knees trembled violently, threatening to dump me onto the ground. I gripped the trunk of the tree beside me for support. Hoped like hell they didn't hear the leaves rustle.

"That's much better." The bloodthirsty guy pulled the knife out before the man fell to the ground. "Do I need to give you guys lessons in interesting ways to kill people?"

"Nope, we'll leave it to you." The guy who had been restraining the other man clapped him on the back. "Maybe you should write a book."

"I should, shouldn't I?" Mr Bloodthirsty grinned.

"I could call it *One Hundred and One Ways to Eliminate Your Friends and Eviscerate Your Enemies.*"

"Maybe you could shut up. We have to get out of here," the first guy said. "We need to dispose of this." He slipped off his suit jacket and rolled up his sleeves.

I caught a glimpse of the mask he wore on his face. Black with splashes of red here and there. A black feather slanted from the top of either side of the mask, across his forehead.

Simple, but menacing, even without a murder involved. In this context it was fucking terrifying.

"Come on, grab the asshole." He nodded toward the others. They picked up the dead man between them. Grunting under his weight, they hefted him up to waist height.

I pressed myself down lower, until my thighs almost touched the layer of dry leaves on the forest floor. I adjusted my left foot slightly to keep from toppling. My shoe found a twig.

It snapped louder than a stockwhip.

All four of us froze. The four of us that were still alive.

"Is someone there?" the guy with the red and black mask growled, deep and low. A sound that would have been hot as fuck if I wasn't absolutely certain he would cut my throat if he knew I was there. Or maybe I'd end up with a blade in my eye.

Hard pass either way.

"Go and look. We'll take care of this." He barked orders like he expected to be obeyed immediately.

I didn't wait and see who came after me. I rose, picked up my skirt, turned and ran. I headed away from the light of the ballroom, into the deepening shadows. My heart raced harder than ever.

Every passing second, I expected someone to explode out of the trees behind me and catch me.

Years of gymnastics and aerial silks meant I was graceful, but I was also terrified. And more or less running blind. Any moment now, I'd trip over a stick or a log and smash my face into the ground. Or my dress would snag on something and tear loudly. Or—

"I know you're there," a sing-song voice called out behind me. "I know what you saw. Why don't you stop and let us talk about it?"

Oh, fuck nope.

I trotted behind a tree and ducked down low. My palms were slick with sweat and I was about ready to piss myself too. I forced deep, measured breaths in and out, to keep myself from holding it. Nothing would give me away like passing out and crashing onto the ground.

Footsteps approached. The snap of a twig, the swish of a branch, the soft murmur of leaves under his shoes.

Crunch.

Crunch.

Crunch.

"I could turn on my phone and find you," he said easily. "But where's the fun in that? The thrill of the chase is much more entertaining. Then when I catch you, I'll know I've earned my trophy." He rubbed his palms on each other.

Oh good, I was going to end up one of those stuffed heads people have on their walls. He might have a collection of them. One hundred and one for every way he knew to kill.

I pressed myself down smaller and closed my eyes. I was even more grateful now that I wore a dark dress and not pale pink. That would have stood out like the proverbial dog's balls, even in the middle of the night.

"I know I'm supposed to find you, and catch you, but you know what, I don't think I will right now." He sounded like he was turning around in a slow circle. "I think, sooner or later, I will find you. You'll come to me and then we'll deal with you. I'm going to enjoy knowing you'll spend every day wondering if this will be the day when I catch my prey. If this will be the day when you end up in my trap. If this is the day I make you mine. I'm going to enjoy making you squeal, little mouse."

My mouth went dry. What kind of twisted, sick fuck was this? Oh yeah, one who liked to stab people in the eye. I had a feeling that, given the chance, he'd take his time, make the man suffer before he died. One thing I knew for certain was, I didn't want to end up that way.

"They're going to be pissed off I let you go, but don't worry. I'll deal with them. I know just the way to handle them, like I know how to handle you. You're probably thinking I don't have a clue, but I know more than you might imagine. Such a sweet perfume, little mouse. I don't mean the stuff you dabbed on behind your ears and on your wrists. I mean the scent of you. Your pussy. Your arousal. Your *fear*."

He took a long, slow sniff of the air. "Intoxicating."

Oh God, this guy was out of his mind. There was no way he could really smell me, was there? Okay, maybe my perfume, but not *me*. Not how scared I was.

No, he was guessing. It wasn't much of a stretch.

I was hiding in the dark from someone who murdered another person. Whose friends were out there, disposing of the body.

How would they do it? They probably had one hundred and one ways of getting rid of a corpse. Would I be one hundred and two? Would they dig me a shallow grave in the forest and leave me there, dusting dirt off their hands? They wouldn't give me a second thought after that. While I decomposed down to my bones, they'd get on with their lives, doing whatever shit they did.

I had to stop thinking this way, it was making my fear worse. If he couldn't smell me before, he would if I kept going like this. I tried to calm my racing mind. He didn't know where I was or who I was. Once he walked away, he wouldn't find me. I might change my perfume, just in case, but otherwise his game would go unplayed. There would be no hunt, no prey, no trophy. All I had to do was stay calm and not freak out. Freaking out would definitely give me away, like waving a huge red flag while standing in the middle of the road.

"I'll see you soon, little mouse," he said. "Or maybe it will be later. Now I think about it, later would be better. Your fear will taste sweeter then. Like honey and wine. Like the smoothest chocolate melted down until it's liquid. Like cum. Perfect for drinking." He smacked his lips and turned to disappear into the trees.

I stayed crouched there for a long time, listening to the distant music, the lap of waves against the side of the lake, the whisper of the breeze and the pounding of my heart.

CHAPTER TWO

KENNEDY

"Isn't it just wonderful here?" My mother spread her hands and gestured at the view out the window.

Helen Knight had expensive taste. She always had. Nothing but the best homes in the best neighbourhoods, with the best schools, reached by driving the best cars. Apparently, my father made sure we were well taken care of, even though he was absent from my life.

My mother made sure to spend as much of what he gave her as she could. All of the luxury I grew up with was nothing compared to this.

The house was huge, set in ten of the best acres in Dusk Bay. On one side were elaborate gardens and an enormous swimming pool. On the other was a cliff with a sheer drop and stunning view of the ocean.

"It's fine," I said vaguely, only half hearing the question. It was probably something wedding related. I didn't know why she asked me. Whatever answer I gave, she already made up her mind anyway. In the end, smiling, nodding and agreeing was the only way to go.

Not to mention I couldn't stop thinking about the other night. Over and over in my mind like a constant, instant replay. Blood spurted out of the man's neck. The twist of the knife in his eye. The guy who stood so close to me in the dark and claimed he'd find me. It was all I could think about when I was awake. All I dreamt about when I was asleep. The knife, the mask tattoo, the blood. Everything blurred together in my mind except the fear. That lingered like it happened moments ago.

Mum looked at me sharply. "What's wrong with you lately, Kennedy? Every time I try to talk to you, it feels like you're on another planet."

She was right, I was and unless I wanted to answer a pile of questions I had no answers for, I was going to have to pretend nothing was wrong. What in the world would I say anyway? The three masked guys killed a man. They didn't know who I was. I didn't know who they were either. If I went to the police, I suspected they wouldn't find a body. Or any sign of a struggle. No proof anything happened, except my word. I risked leaving the killers a trail that would lead straight to me.

I had no choice but to keep quiet.

I forced a smile. "I'm sorry, I was just thinking about what UNI classes I need to take."

That was a flat out lie and we both knew it. I was in the final year of my computer science degree. I knew exactly what I needed to take to finish.

At Mum's insistence, I'd agreed to complete my final year here at Dusk Bay instead of on campus. A decision I was starting to regret. As far as I knew, no one on campus was a murderer. None I was witness to anyway.

A flicker of movement out the window caught my eye. The massive iron gates that led into the property opened slowly. Before it was open wide enough, a sleek black SUV rolled inside.

I winced, but it slid through effortlessly and came to a stop outside. The driver must have missed hitting the iron by a hair or two on either side.

The guy that climbed out of the passenger seat had a scowl etched on his face, like somehow it might be his permanent expression. His hair was blond and short, slightly longer on the top than on the sides. His square jaw was covered with a light smattering of stubble. Both his face and body looked like they were carved out of stone, cold and hard. A dark blue T-shirt clung to broad shoulders and chest, and flat stomach. I bet myself he had abs for days, but his face was all, 'don't fucking touch me.'

So, of course, that was exactly what I wanted to do.

The driver looked just as cut, but where the first guy was blond and blue-eyed, this guy had dark hair and dark eyes. The kind that could see right through you, because he can't be bothered to look *at* you. His white T-shirt contrasted with tanned skin. I couldn't help wondering what he'd look like if that T-shirt was wet and clinging to every dip and groove of his body. Droplets of water cascading from his hair and face when he shook his head. His...

That thought made my mouth dry and sent a rush of warmth through my body.

I swallowed hard.

A third guy got out of the back of the car. The sides of his mouth turned up in a smile. He said something to the blond, and got a glance in return, but no other response. For some reason, that made him grin. He pushed dark hair out of his eyes and moved around to the back of the car to open it and pull out a suitcase. To go with his dark hair, he was dressed completely in black. A t-shirt like the other two, over ripped jeans. His hair was pulled back in a bun.

Unlike the other two guys, he looked completely at home.

"Please say he's my stepbrother-to-be," I muttered. According to Mum, he'd just finished his degree at Brutham Academy and was returning to Dusk Bay to work for his father.

The guy with the white T-shirt stepped around and yanked the handle of the suitcase out of the other guy's hand before rolling it towards the house.

Crap. Of course it couldn't be the guy who actually looked friendly.

My mother hurried over to the door to greet them, but I hung back.

"Mannix!" She greeted him with open arms.

He gave her the shortest hug in human history, before stepping aside to let the other guys enter.

"Helen." He nodded towards the blond. "Ares." Then to man bun. "Isaac."

Isaac grinned and held out his hand to Mum. "Everyone calls me Ice. It's nice to meet you."

"It's nice to meet you too, Isaac," Mum said.

Apparently, 'everybody,' didn't apply to her. She turned to look at me and waved me forward.

"This is my daughter, Kennedy Knight."

I didn't miss the way all of the guys raked up and down my body with their eyes. Or the way Ares curled his lip at me. Ice regarded me with interest. Mannix's expression was unreadable, but he carried an air of annoyance at my existence.

Ice surprised me by stepping forward and grabbing me up in a bear hug. "Don't mind those two. They'll be nice when they get their heads out of their asses."

I hugged him back. He smelled nice, like a combination of musk and cinnamon.

"When will that be?" I asked sweetly.

Ice chuckled. "Hopefully some time this decade, before they suffocate on their own shit."

"Fuck off," Ares growled. "Not everyone likes annoyingly cheerful." His sneer seemed to be the default expression every time he looked at me. Although, he looked at Ice the same way. Maybe he was just a dick.

"My theory is that he got out on the wrong side of the bed about twenty years ago," Ice whispered loudly to me.

Ares flipped him off.

"Is my father around?" Apparently Mannix was done with the pleasantries. If you could call them that.

"He's upstairs in his office," Mum said. She didn't seem concerned at any of their attitudes. Then again, she was so deliriously happy with Leo, she probably wouldn't notice if the world ended right in front of her face.

"I need to talk to him, then I'll drive you clowns home," Mannix said.

"I could drive Ares home," Ice offered.

Mannix and Ares both said, "No!" At the same time.

"The last time you drove, we ended up in a ditch," Ares growled.

Ice shrugged. "Practice makes perfect. How am I supposed to get perfect if you don't let me practice?"

"Practice in your own car," Mannix said.

Ice reached into his back pocket and pulled out his wallet. He opened it and grabbed hold of a credit card between his thumb and forefinger. He held out to Mannix.

Mannix looked at him funny. "What the fuck are you doing?"

"Buying your car," Ice said easily. "Then I can

drive my own car. And you can buy yourself a new one tomorrow. Win-win."

Rich boy problems. I knew Mum loved Leo, but I suspected she also loved the fact he had more money than God. So did Mannix, and apparently his friends. I couldn't even imagine buying a car on a whim. Even if I could afford it, I liked to think things through.

Mannix shook his head and turned to hurry up the stairs. His feet thumped heavily all the way to the top, like he was announcing his presence with each step. Or trying to break through to the space under the stairs.

Ares leaned against a wall and crossed his arms over his ridiculously broad chest. He'd be hot if he wasn't looking at me like something the cat dragged in.

Yeah, fuck you too, asshole.

Ice slipped his credit card back into his wallet and shoved it back in his pocket. "I guess I'll go car shopping tomorrow. Wanna come?" he asked me.

"She's probably busy," Ares snapped.

Ice's eyes were still on me, when he said, "Doing what?"

Before I could answer, Ares said, "Washing her hair or getting her nails done. Some shit like that."

I glanced down at my natural, bitten nails. I'd never had acrylic on them in my life. As for washing my hair...

"What is your problem?" I asked him. "I met you approximately three minutes ago and you've already decided you don't like me?" Apart from wondering how his tongue would feel on my clit, the feeling was mutual. I'd bet half my trust fund that his cock would fill me up and then some. Ugh, I needed to stop that line of thought right now. If I didn't, I was going to drip on the hardwood floor.

"Kennedy," Mum hissed, as though I was the antagonist in all of this. "Let's not have any unpleasantness. Perhaps we can all get some coffee. I'm sure we would all get along if we got to know each other."

Ares gave me a sarcastic smirk.

I badly wanted to flip him off, or better yet, kick him in the balls, but I didn't want to upset Mum. Thank fuck he didn't live here. With any luck, I wouldn't have to see much of him or Mannix.

Ice seemed okay, if a bit strange, but if hanging out with him meant hanging out with them, I'd have to pass. Just because they were all hot didn't mean I had to give them the time of day. I needed to find my own friends, which meant going to the gymnastics studio to see if I could spend some time in the gym.

With any luck, I'd meet a hot coach and forget all about these three guys.

"I could go for a coffee," Ice said cheerfully. "Knowing Mannix, talking to Leo will take ages. And may or may not involve one or both of them bleeding."

I snorted a soft laugh. At least, I thought he was joking. My stepfather-to-be was nice enough, but he was intense. Like Mannix, he had an undercurrent of something dark. Like if you lifted the lid, you'd find a rolling boil of violence. He'd never hurt my mother, but other people? If anyone lay a hand on her without her permission, he'd want to rip their arms off and shove them down their throat.

It was... Sweet. Would he act on that though?

That brought me back to that night and the tang of blood and death. It wasn't just that night, I realised. Dusk Bay had a feeling about it. Like it was teetering on the edge. On the edge of what, I had no idea, but I had a very strong feeling I should be scared of it.

CHAPTER THREE

"So much for not seeing them," I muttered under my breath.

For people who didn't live here, Ice and Ares were here all the time. As far as I could tell, they both lived a handful of minutes away, but whenever I saw Mannix, they were with him. Ice was friendly enough, but the other two hadn't thawed a drop. Ironic that they were colder than he was.

They must have heard me mutter, because Ares turned to give me his customary sneer.

Mannix matched it with his usual annoyance at my presence.

Okay, I got it. This was his house and I wasn't even legally a stepsibling. I was just the daughter of his father's fiancée. Still, did he have to look at me like I was trespassing?

"Hey, what are you doing?" Ice slipped into the chair next to me. He didn't even pretend he wasn't looking at my laptop screen. "Oh, essay writing. Yeah, I don't miss that."

"I'm sure you don't." I closed my laptop and tried not to look at Mannix when he gripped the hem of his T-shirt and pulled it off over his head with one hand. Why the hell was it so hot when guys did that?

On the other hand, did he have to strip off right in front of me? I was supposed to be concentrating on university work, not counting his abs—eight—or admiring the V of his hips. I really shouldn't be memorising his tattoos, or how fucking thick his biceps were. Or the way his thighs looked like he could crush a watermelon without raising a sweat.

Crap, I was wetter than the pool right in front of me.

I could study in my room, but it was a nice day to sit under a wide umbrella beside the sparkling water. Right, I was only here for the pool, not the view of the guys when they came out at the same time every morning for a swim. I totally didn't work here so I could watch them do laps and splash each other, all shirtless and hot.

"Ice," Ares growled. He looked at me like somehow I'd be a bad influence on his friend.

I met his gaze glare for glare until his eyes slid away like I wasn't worthy of another second of his time. If he thought I'd be intimidated, he'd have to think again.

He pulled off his T-shirt and threw it across the back of a chair. He dove into the pool right in front of me, clearly knowing he'd leave a splash behind.

"Asshole." I grabbed my laptop and turned so it didn't get wet. If it did, the fucker could buy me a new one. Yeah, hell would freeze over before he did that.

Mannix grinned. Apparently the sight of me pissed off amused him somehow.

I resisted the urge to flip him off.

Don't take their bait, I told myself. For some reason, they seemed to have made it their life's goal to make me as unwelcome as possible. I wasn't going to let them get to me. Right now, this was as much my home as it was Mannix's.

"How are you friends with these assholes?" I asked as Mannix leapt into the water, his arms around his knees. The splash from his bomb sent droplets of water flying, covering the top of the table.

If I hadn't moved my laptop, it would have gotten drenched.

Ice shrugged. "They're okay when you get to know them."

"How will I do that when they don't want to know me?" Did I really want to anyway? I should at least try to get to know Mannix, if only for my mother's sake. I owed Ares no such consideration. If anything, I owed him a big, fat fuck you.

"If they don't, then I get more time with you," he reasoned.

I brushed a tangle of red hair off my face and looked at him in surprise. "At least one of you is nice." He wanted to spend time with me? His friends would love that. Not.

He smiled, which was just as panty melting as any set of abs, but said, "Don't be fooled. I'm nowhere near as nice as I seem. If anything, I'm less nice and more dangerous than those two clowns." He jerked a thumb in the direction of Ares and Mannix, who were freestyling neck and neck up and down the pool.

I'd seen their routine often enough to have it memorised. They started with a few laps of freestyle before switching to butterfly, then backstroke and finally to breaststroke to cool down.

"I don't know, you seem a lot nicer than them. Did you meet on the swim team or something?" They all seemed to know how to do the strokes correctly. At least, as far as I could tell. I was no expert on swimming techniques.

"Something like that," Ice said. "We all like getting wet." He gave me a smile that left me in no doubt about what he was referring to.

Hint: nothing to do with pool water. Or any other kind of water for that matter.

My face heated, which made him smile wider. He also liked to get to me, but in a different way from the other two. It was hard enough to focus with them around, without one of them flirting with me.

"I'm sure you do," I said awkwardly. "Shouldn't you be swimming too?"

"Yes, I should." He hopped up, but before he walked away, he leaned over to whisper in my ear, "Are you wet already, Beautiful?" His warm breath brushed the side of my neck. My skin pebbled. So did my nipples.

Before I could answer, he straightened up, winked and walked away to the other side of the pool before stripping off his shirt and diving in.

He might be right about being dangerous, especially to my heart rate. More than that though. He also had a simmering undercurrent of violence, but kept it behind a friendlier mask.

The thought of masks took me back to that night and my pulse quickened.

Dusk Bay was a combination of violence and sex that shouldn't be heady, but it was.

Not the murder, that was terrifying, but the sense that three guys doing laps across the pool in front of me knew how to use their bodies to hurt other people. Fists, feet, thighs. My money would be on them in a fight. What if they fought each other? I didn't know who'd win, but imagining them wrestling made me hotter than hell.

I scooped up my laptop from my lap and glanced down at the table. I sighed. The surface was too wet to put my computer back down. As tempting as it was—and it really was—to pick up Ares' t-shirt from the back of the chair and wipe the table with it, I decided I didn't need him hating me more than he already did.

I couldn't stop him from being an asshole, but I didn't need to be one as well.

Reluctantly, I stood and carried my laptop inside. I set it down on the kitchen island and opened it. Before I slipped into a stool, I glanced back at the door. Through the clear glass, Mannix watched me.

A hint of a frown was etched on his brow. When he saw me looking, he turned away and disappeared under the water.

What the fuck was that frown for? Had he and Ares deliberately wet the table to drive me away? Was Mannix pissed off it hadn't driven me far enough? Maybe he wouldn't be happy until I moved out, or left Dusk Bay.

If that was the petty game he and his friends were playing then too bad. I wasn't going anywhere. For one thing, Leo's house had the best Wi-Fi I'd ever had access to. It was crazy fast and strong everywhere in the house.

Yeah, for good Wi-Fi, I'll put up with the occasional hostile glance. Priorities.

Besides, the guys were assholes, but they were good to look at. Ice was right, I got wet around them. Especially when they took their shirts off. There was definitely danger in that. Being attracted to guys who hated my guts would get me nowhere.

I sighed and flipped open my laptop. I opened a search window and typed in gymnastic studios nearby. There was one in town. According to their website, they had aerial silks for me to practice on. Hell yeah. A lot didn't, since it wasn't a recognised gymnastics apparatus.

I grabbed my phone out of my pocket and shot off a text message about renting the gym or doing a class. Whatever it took, as long as I got to practice. It was that or ask Leo to bolt some silks to the top of the staircase. If Mum asked, he'd probably do just that, but I wasn't going to meet any hot coaches if I stayed here. Just hot assholes who weren't worth my time.

I closed the web browser and opened my essay file. Information security analytics might be as boring as hell to a lot of people, but it fascinated me. Every day it seemed like another big corporation was hacked. When I finished my degree, I wanted to prevent those hackings. Companies owed it to their customers to keep their information safe, not let it be sold on the dark web. Maybe I was an idealist, thinking I could actually prevent cyber attacks, but at least I could help to minimise them, and clean up afterwards.

All of that was shorthand for, Kennedy Knight is a massive nerd. A nerd who would get a lucrative job after I graduated. There was nothing to be ashamed of here.

I read over my work, making corrections here and there before I started on the conclusion. I was so absorbed in my work I didn't notice the guys got out of the pool until the door slid open behind me and they strutted inside like all three of them owned the place.

I kept my gaze on the screen, but watched them move around in the corner of my eye.

Mannix went to the fridge and pulled out drinks for the other two and himself. They all twisted off the caps and tossed them down on the island next to my laptop.

They were obviously trying to piss me off, so I ignored them.

"Are we going to that party tonight?" Ares asked.

That was obvious too. He wanted me to know they were invited and I wasn't. Whatever.

I had more important things to worry about than their petty games. Although, a party would be fun and a good way to meet people.

I tapped my keyboard as though I hadn't heard.

Mannix leaned his elbows on the island and looked right at me. "I think we should."

"We should take Kennedy with us," Ice said.

Ares and Mannix both stiffened.

"You want to come, don't you, Kennedy?" Ice slid a hand under my hair and rested it lightly on the back of my neck.

Luckily I was sitting, because his touch set me on

fire and made my knees weak. My breath hitched. I know they all heard it.

Which kind of come did he mean? To the party, or orgasm? Of course, he probably meant both, and that would have been my answer if I could speak coherently.

"She's not invited," Ares snapped.

"She's invited if we bring her," Ice said easily. "You want to come, Kennedy?" He squeezed the back of my neck and I had the strangest sensation that he wanted to wrap his fingers around my throat and squeeze. And squeeze until the light left my eyes.

I was terrified and turned on at the same time.

"I'd love to," I said finally.

I ignored Ares' growl of irritation. And the deepening frown on Mannix's gorgeous face.

I hope like hell I didn't live to regret agreeing to go.

CHAPTER FOUR

MANNIX

"Why the fuck did you invite her?" I growled. "What part of *she's not fucking invited* did you not get?"

It was typical of Ice to invite first and give a shit about the consequences later. Or not at all. Right now, he didn't seem to give a crap about the bomb he threw in the middle of the three of us. Girls like Kennedy Knight and her mother were nothing but trouble. Women in general.

Kennedy, in particular, was too fucking cute for her own good. The moment I first laid eyes on her, I wanted to tear her clothes off and slam my cock into her wet heat. I bet anything she was tight. Girls like her always were. The ones who went about pretending they had no idea how fucking hot they were. But they knew. They always did. Why else would she walk around my home in a singlet and tight little shorts? She might as well be waving a flag with the words, 'bend me over and fuck me,' written on it.

And I wanted to. That was a problem. Especially in light of the fact Ares and Ice also wanted to bounce her on their cock. The guys were my brothers, but I didn't want to fucking share.

No, the best thing I could do was stay as far away as I could from Kennedy fucking Knight and her perfect tits. At least until the other guys lost interest, because my pretty little stepsister-to-be was *mine*. I couldn't wait to teach her the way I like my cock sucked. The thought of her mouth, her throat, made me hard.

"I invited her because I wanted her to come," Ice said unapologetically. "All study and no play..." He waved a hand in the air. "Blah blah blah. You wouldn't want the Cassani family to get a reputation for being boring, do you?"

I grunted in response. "Like that will happen. No one would dare say shit like that about us." They wouldn't because either I'd kill them or I'd have one of my father's people do it.

Everyone in Dusk Bay knew that. We didn't have quite the power of the DiMarco family, who ran the city, or the Brantley family, who ran the state, but my father was a loyal minion of them both. Ric DiMarco and Caleb Brantley trusted him as much as they trusted anyone. And by extension, they trusted me.

I knew more about my father's business than anyone except him and my older brother Gunnar. Whatever was asked of him, of us, we'd do it. Anything from running guns and drugs to trafficking diamonds and even people.

"The bitch is trouble," Ares said. Like Ice, his family were local to Dusk Bay. More loyal minions of Ric and Caleb. The three of us went to school together, then went away to Brutham Academy. Brutal Academy, they call it. If you make it through your first year there alive, you have at least a fifty-fifty chance of surviving until graduation.

First year exams include hunting down other students by any means necessary. It was a perfect opportunity to get rid of any threats who would pose a problem at some point in the future. I was hunted by a member of the Bell family, who took it upon herself to rid the world of any threats to them. I can still feel my hands around her throat, squeezing until her body went still and the last breath slipped from between her lips. Shame, she had one of the tightest pussies I'd ever fucked. She made her choice when she chose the wrong side. She deserved a slower death than what I gave her, but I couldn't take the chance she was working with someone else. It was her or me and it wasn't going to be me.

"She's almost harmless," Ice said.

Ares grunted. "She's either harmless or she's not. And she's not. She's a ticking time bomb in the middle of a field of sheep."

I cut him a look. "A field of sheep, bro? Do I look furry to you?"

"Isn't it fleece?" Ice asked.

"Whatever," I grunted. "Either way, I'm no lamb." Kennedy might be though. A sweet little lamb, ready to be led right to her own slaughter. After I fucked her until her body was boneless. Until she begged me to stop. No, I'd still keep going. I wanted to make her cry. I wanted her so sore she couldn't walk for a week. For a month. When she couldn't take any more of me, I'd still give her more. When I was done, she would know exactly who she belonged to. Who owned her.

"She's a pain in the ass and the sooner she gets the hell out of Dusk Bay, the better," Ares growled. "The better for us and the better for her." His blue eyes were dark with anger or lust, or a combination of the two. Ever since I've known him, he was a dark and complicated guy. I could count on one hand the amount of times I saw him smile. According to him, he was born fucked up. That sounded accurate to me.

"The better for us and the better for her," he said again.

Usually, I agreed with him, but not on this. Kennedy wasn't leaving. I wouldn't allow it. If she tried, I'd hunt her down and bring her back, whether she wanted to return or not.

Thing is, I knew he didn't want her to leave either. I saw the way he looked at her. He was already mentally pinning her down under the weight of his body and slamming his cock into her.

I curled my hands into fists under the table and kept them there to stop myself from punching Ares in the face. It wasn't his fault he was hot for her, but I needed to find him someone else to obsess over. Ice too. Him being nice to her, touching her, that was also a problem. I wanted to push him into the pool and hold him under until he stopped kicking.

I wouldn't though, because he was my brother. Both of them had short attention spans when it came to women. In a week or two, they'd be drooling over someone else and leaving me to make my move.

I glanced over to where she sat, talking to Daisy

Lasalle, of all people. Known by most people in Dusk Bay as Daze, she was my older brother's girlfriend. At the same time, she's screwing Ric DiMarco and Caleb Brantley's right-hand man, Hilton Blake. She was as powerful as any of them, as deadly. Anyone who crossed any of her boyfriends, or her, would wish for death, instead of the slow torture they'd inflict on them.

Anyone with half a brain was scared of her. Including me. Right now, she was smiling and laughing at something Kennedy said. I couldn't tell if the two women becoming friends would be a good thing or the worst idea ever. I had no trouble telling Kennedy who she could and couldn't be friends with, except for Daisy Lasalle. If I wanted to keep my cock intact, I'd stay out of that. As it happens, I'm very attached to my cock.

"See, she's making friends already." Ice nodded toward the pair. He smiled like an indulgent father who was happy his toddler was playing nicely in the sandpit with another kid. Or sharing the red finger paint.

"Perfect." Ares scowled but he said, "If Daze doesn't scare her into running out of town, nothing will. Any minute now she'll start telling Kennedy how she likes to ask her boyfriends to break thumbs for her. Or about the time she and Ric locked a guy in his own cool room to die slowly."

I smiled. That was pretty epic. From what I've heard, the cool room walls and door were too thick for anyone to hear him shouting. Who knows whether he froze or suffocated. Either way, it wasn't a quick and cheerful death. I doubted Daze or Ric lost any sleep over it. Knowing those two, they probably talked and laughed about it while they fucked. Judging by the fact he always had half-healed knife wounds on his neck, things got wild at their place.

I won't lie, I'd stick my cock into her if I got the chance. Most of the guys in Dusk Bay would. They'd probably lose their cock five seconds later, but it might just be worth it.

"Do you think she knows what this place is like?" Ice propped his elbow on the table and rested his chin on his hand. His hazel eyes lingered on Kennedy. "I mean, she seems innocent to me. Like she thinks we all have pet bunnies, and spend our weekends mowing lawns and growing chrysanthemums."

"You did have a pet bunny and grew chrysanthemums," I pointed out. His parents paid someone to mow the lawn.

He looked over at me, a dreamy expression on his

face. "Yeah, Mr Flopsy. I was so sad when he died. But then I got to cut him up and see how he worked." The memory of that brightened him up a little. Typical Ice. I'd seen him slice animals and people and marvel at the blood, bones and muscles and the way everything fit together, and came apart. No wonder he studied forensic pathology at university. He loved nothing better than a good autopsy.

Sick fuck.

I wasn't entirely convinced Mr Flopsy hadn't met with a nasty Ice-related accident, but he seemed genuinely upset when the thing died. Maybe he'd killed it by accident. If he had, it was the only time he ever killed anything or anyone by accident. It might have given him a taste of blood and death. A thirst he enjoyed slaking whenever he could. I've never met anyone who enjoyed killing as much as he did. It was almost like he needed to murder someone to start his day, like normal people drank coffee.

"Did you dissect the chrysanthemums too?" Ares asked, his tone scathing.

Ice cocked his head at him. "No, those were for my mother. She liked to have fresh flowers every-where." A mischievous glint in his eye added, "Your mother liked them too, right before I—"

Ares growled deep in the back of his throat.

"Don't try to imply you fucked my mother. I'll rip off your dick and shove it down your throat."

"I wasn't trying to imply anything," Ice said as though he was saying it outright. He probably had fucked Ares' mother. Almost everyone else in Dusk Bay had, except me. I wasn't into older women who liked to be in control. I preferred to be the one in control.

"You're an asshole," Ares said.

"Maybe, but I..."

I tuned out their bullshit and looked around the party as though I wasn't keeping a close eye on Kennedy. I made a note of everyone she spoke to, especially anyone she was friendly with. Particularly if they had a cock. If they thought they were going to touch her, they could think again.

I'd cut their fucking hand off and smack them with it, then stab them in the stomach and let them die slowly. I'd make Kennedy watch so she knew what would happen to anyone if she let them touch her. Then I'd tie her to my bed and punish her by making her ass black and blue with my hand before I fucked the hell out of her.

Everyone would learn not to touch her. Including her. By the time I was done with her, she'd know not to touch herself. I'd be the only one to touch her, to get her off.

Me.

And when she came, she'd scream my name and be grateful to belong to me.

CHAPTER FIVE

KENNEDY

"So... I'm supposed to go in this morning to check out the gymnastics place," I said slowly.

Mum and Leo both looked at me over their coffee cups. Their expressions matched except for Leo's slightly raised eyebrow.

"I don't have a car." I thought back to Ice offering to buy Mannix's car like it was nothing. It was probably nothing for Leo too, but I wanted to buy my own car when I had my own money. I hadn't needed one back in Sydney, I took the train everywhere, or rode my bike. Public transport didn't come to this part of Dusk Bay. And it was too far from anywhere to ride.

"If I could borrow one..." I started tentatively. Leo had a collection of them, but most of them were crazy expensive, like his white Shelby Cobra, and a classic Rolls-Royce. All I needed was an old rust bucket. Or a little hatchback.

"I'll drive you," Mannix said, his voice tight. He was standing in the kitchen, his back to the bench. His long fingers were curled around a black mug full of black coffee. The same shade as his soul.

He gave me a look like I'd insisted, instead of him offering.

"What a lovely idea," Mum said. "It's so nice to see you two getting along."

I gave her a watery smile. He let me tag along to the party, but didn't say a word to me all night, or since. It seemed like every time I turned around, he was watching me, trying to figure out a way to get rid of me. Every time I caught him looking, he immediately looked away and stalked off into another room.

Mannix looked at Mum like maybe she was crazy, but didn't say anything. It was obvious to everyone we weren't exactly friends.

That begged the question of why he offered to drive me in the first place. Was this his attempt to make an effort to get to know me, or was I going to end up disposed of, like the man at the ball?

Yeah, okay, I was being a little bit paranoid, but I *had* seen a man murdered. Part of me wanted to ask if Mannix knew anything about it, but he and his friends weren't in town at the time. Did Leo know? Did I want to know if he did?

No, that was something better not discussed, not thought about. Forgetting was easier said than done though. My nightmares were still full of blood and masks.

"I have to go into town anyway." Mannix shrugged. There was that look again, like somehow he thought I was making him drive.

"I don't want to be a hassle—" I started.

Mannix put his coffee cup down on the bench hard enough to make me jump. He smirked. Apparently making me startle was hilarious and intentional.

Asshole.

"Like I said, I'm going anyway. If you want a ride, you have five minutes." He scooped up his cup and put it in the dishwasher.

"Five minutes sounds accurate," I told him as I put my bowl and mug in the dishwasher beside his cup. I gave him a sweet smile when he scowled at me.

"It would still be the best five minutes of your life." He gave me a dark look and strode away toward the garage.

"Dream on," I said under my breath. He might be hot, and sexy, and the thought of him touching me set my blood on fire, but he was still a jerk and my stepbrother-to-be.

I hurried off to change into leggings and a loose T-shirt. I shoved my feet into running shoes and trotted down the stairs as Mannix backed the SUV out of the garage. I thought he might drive off without me, but he stopped long enough for me to slip into the passenger seat. I barely got the door closed before he gunned the engine and flew down the gravel driveway. I managed to drag my seatbelt over me and click it into place before he braked heavily and waited for the gate to open.

"Thanks for offering to drive me." Maybe if I was nice to him, he'd be less of a dick back to me.

A girl could hope, right?

"If I hadn't, Dad would have spent my inheritance buying you a car," he said.

"I never would have expected him to do that."

"He'd still do it, whether you expect it or not." He accelerated hard and the SUV jumped past the gate and onto the road.

I sighed because he was probably right, but I couldn't help that.

"I don't want his money or yours," I said firmly. "I

can make my own money. I don't need to live off a parent or stepparent." Wasn't he doing exactly that? Daddy gave him a job. Leo probably brought him this SUV. He got to live in a mansion and be a jerk all day with his asshole friends.

Mannix snorted with disbelief. "So if we get home and one of those cute little bright pink cars with a pretty little pink ribbon around it was there, you're gonna say no to it?"

Pink wasn't my favourite colour, but it would be difficult to refuse a gift like that. "I don't—"

"Of course you're not going to fucking say no," he snarled. "Girls like you don't get anywhere if they say no."

I glared over at him. "What's that supposed to mean? If you're trying to suggest I haven't worked hard at university, or at—"

He cut off a white van and flipped the driver off out the window. "Learn to drive, dickhead."

He glanced over at me. "I'm saying girls like you want to say yes. You get off on making people happy. Don't tell me I'm wrong, because we both know I'm not."

He wasn't wrong. But was it bad to be a people pleaser?

"What does that make you?" I asked. "The kind of

guy who gets off on telling people no for no reason? Who won't give an inch, even if it's in your best interest to do it?"

He shrugged one shoulder. "Maybe. It's better than being a pushover."

"Is it?" I challenged him. "Seems like being a nice person makes life easier for everyone, especially myself."

"An easy life is an illusion. The world is a shit hole. No amount of nice is going to change that, it just gets you screwed over." He seemed to be speaking from experience.

"Who hurt you?" I asked. "Aren't you a bit young to be that cynical?"

He stopped the SUV at a traffic light and cut me a look and a bitter smile. "I'm not cynical, I'm a realist. The universe isn't sitting there waiting to give you what you want. The only way to really get what you want and what you need is to fucking take it. That's why if Dad gives you a car, you'll accept. Even if the car comes with a blowjob."

I grimaced. "I definitely wouldn't take it if it did. And Leo wouldn't cheat on my mother."

"Who said he'd be the one to receive the blowjob?" Mannix gave me a look like he'd happily drag my face down to his lap and make me suck him off while he drove.

"Does your family often give gifts with conditions attached?" I asked.

"Frequently." The light turned green and he turned his attention back to the road. "No one in the world gives gifts without strings attached. There's no such thing as a free blowjob."

"You should get that on a T-shirt," I said dryly. "Maybe sell them at the local market. You might make a few dollars. I'm sure Ares and Ice would come and help you out." Ares and Mannix would scare all the customers away, but Ice might sell a few. If nothing else, it was an interesting mental image.

"I'll save one for you," Mannix said. "A white one that's tight around your tits. No bra. You could make a few dollars giving paid blowjobs. I'd be first in line."

I believed him. He hated my guts, but he'd enjoy seeing me on my knees, my lips around his cock. His eyes on mine as I sucked his thick length. His hips moving slowly back and forth, grunts of pleasure slipping from his mouth.

I shook my head to get the thought out of it. I should one hundred percent not be thinking about him like this. He might not appreciate it if I left a puddle on his seat, even if it was because I was thinking inappropriate thoughts about my step-brother-to-be.

"I know I need money for a car, but I'm not that desperate." I adjusted my position on the seat.

"Yet," he said.

"I have no plans to be that desperate ever," I retorted. I wouldn't knock anyone who was employed in the sex industry, but it wasn't a career I aspired to have.

"Shame, I hear it pays well."

"If you're so worried about Leo giving away your inheritance, maybe you should look into it for yourself. I'm sure you'd be popular." Lonely, rich housewives would probably pay a ton to fuck him. Men too.

"No one would be able to afford me." He looked smug.

I snorted. At least we were getting along with each other now, more or less. This was the first halfway decent conversation we had since we met. This might be as good as we got with each other.

He pulled up in front of the gymnastic studio and killed the engine.

"I'll be back in an hour. That should be long enough for you to do your shit." He was telling, not asking. If I wasn't ready to go when he got back, I'd have to find my own way back home. He wouldn't regret leaving me behind for a moment.

"An hour should be plenty," I said lightly. "Thank you again for—"

"Are you going to get out sometime today?" His inpatient tone matched the dark look in his eyes. Evidently he'd exhausted his quota of pleasantry, and was done with me.

Our tentative peace was at an end.

"Yeah." I pushed the door open and climbed out. I'd barely shut the door behind me when he pulled away from the curb and roared off down the street. I was lucky he didn't run over my feet. That was probably his plan.

Not today, motherfucker.

Why did he have to be so fucking hot and an asshole at the same time? Had something terrible happened to make him so cynical? Maybe he witnessed a murder too. Seeing that, living with the memory, would mess with anyone's mind. It was certainly messing with mine. I considered therapy, but dismissed the idea. I couldn't talk about it without risking giving away details. As much as I'd like to trust a therapist to keep things confidential, I'd be naïve to think the chance of details getting out was zero.

"I'll see you soon, little mouse. Or maybe it will be later. Now I think about it, later would be better. Your fear will taste sweeter then. Like honey and wine. Like the smoothest chocolate melted down until it's liquid. Like cum. Perfect for drinking."

The words were seared into my mind like a brand. I played it over and over again until the idea of melted chocolate made my stomach turn. In my dreams, he took a few steps forward, found me, and tore me open like their victim. Sometimes I dreamt they drank my blood. Sometimes I was still alive when they did it.

If he found me, if *they* found me, I was screwed. Worse than screwed, I'd be dead.

I pushed down the flutter of fear that rose in my chest and stepped through the door and into the gym.

CHAPTER SIX

KENNEDY

This was my happy place. Right at the top of the thick line of bright blue silk.

Technically, stretch polyester, but whatever. I was the most alive with my back arched, hands outstretched, thighs the only part of me gripping the fabric.

I wound the silk around my wrists and let myself drop, face first. I caught myself a couple of centimetres off the mat and grinned at the rush of adrenaline through my body.

A handful of younger gymnasts taking a kid's class stopped to watch, gasped and clapped. Their coach, a guy around my age named Charlie, clapped louder than the kids.

The gruff head coach, Nicola, had palmed me off

to him when I walked through the door. She muttered something about renting out the silks for a couple of hours a week and that she'd consider hiring me to teach. Then she disappeared into her office with a cup of coffee and hadn't emerged since.

I tipped over forward and landed on my feet.

I tugged my t-shirt back into place as Charlie dismissed the class. The kids went running off to their parents who waited near the door.

"It's been a while since we had anyone who could use those." He gave me an easy smile. With sandy blond hair, blue green eyes and the body of a gymnast, it was easy to like Charlie. He was a pleasant change from 'grumpy asshole'.

"I'm a bit rusty," I admitted. "It's been a couple of months since I got to practice."

"If that was rusty, I'd love to see you when you're warmed up and competition fit." He waved back at a couple of the kids as they waved vigorously and giggled. They looked at him with huge eyes that screamed crush.

I got that. If he was my coach, I might have a crush on him too. On paper, he was exactly the kind of guy I should go for, but he didn't get my pulse racing like Mannix and his friends. Figured I wouldn't be into the first nice guy I met since I got to

Dusk Bay. Hopefully he wasn't the only one in town. It would be a long year if he was.

I sighed. "I wish I had time for competition training. At least I can get in some practice here and there." I eyed the clock and then the uneven bars. I had a few minutes before Mannix returned.

"Spot me?" Charlie probably had a life to get to, but he didn't seem to be in a hurry to leave.

"Absolutely." He waited until I chalked my hands and got into place under the lower bar. "Ready?"

I could get up there myself, with the help of the ladder beside the bars, but I decided to let him put his hands around my waist and lift me up to the lower bar. I didn't even mind when his hands lingered a little too long, or the way his toned body felt close to mine.

It was nothing like the rush of heat I got from looking at Mannix, Ares and Ice, but it was pleasant enough.

I started to swing back and forth to build momentum, then leapt onto the higher bar. Back and forth, round and round until everything around me was a blur. I was rusty at this too, but muscle memory took me through a routine I'd practised a billion times. I could even hear the cheesy competition music playing in the back of my mind over and over.

I dropped to my feet, stuck the landing and presented, raising my arms above my head and smiling as Charlie clapped.

"You probably guessed Nicola wanted me to watch you and give her my thoughts on whether or not she should hire you," he said lightly. "She'd be crazy not to. How did you never make the Olympic team?"

"I injured my knee right before the trials." At the time, I was devastated, but that was a few years ago now and I didn't miss the pressure of competitions and the need to succeed. I was happy to do this for fun and maybe for profit if Nicola gave me a job.

Charlie sucked in a breath with sympathy and winced. "That's a bummer. I was never quite good enough. Which is my way of saying I didn't take it seriously. I was too busy clowning around on the rings to win a competition, much less qualify for any big ones." He seemed unworried.

"One more go?" He jerked his head towards the uneven bars.

"I have time for one more." I stepped into the circle of his hands and let him lift me. I'd just gripped the lower bar and started to swing when the door opened with a crash.

I startled so hard my hands slipped and I fell to the mat on my ass. Nothing was hurt but my pride, but that had a pretty big dent in it. I knew better than to react to sudden sounds like that. If I did that during the competition, I'd lose a bunch of points.

Dusk Bay definitely had me on edge.

I looked over to see Mannix standing inside the door, his expression as dark as thunder. He wasn't looking at me. He was looking at Charlie like he wanted to rip his head off and use it as a bowling ball.

I stood up and dusted chalk off my hands. "Looks like my ride is here."

"You know this guy?" Charlie asked uneasily.

That was a good question. Honestly, I hardly knew Mannix at all.

"He's my stepbrother-to-be," I said lightly. "I'll hear from you or Nicola?"

Charlie managed to force his eyes away from Mannix's glare and smiled. "I'd say within a day or two. But you'll be back to practice, yeah?"

I returned his smile. "Definitely, if I can get someone to drive me." I narrowed my eyes at Mannix, hoping he'd get the hint to chill out. I didn't know what his problem with Charlie was and I didn't care. Charlie was a nice guy and hopefully soon a co-worker. Nothing more.

"Hurry up," Mannix snapped. He turned and stomped out the door toward the SUV.

I shrugged at Charlie and grabbed up my stuff before I trotted out after him and slipped into the passenger seat.

Like before, he barely gave me time to close the door and fasten my seatbelt before he pulled away from the curb.

"What is your fucking problem?" I asked him.

"Why was he touching you?" Mannix snapped.

I stared at him. "What?"

"Why. Was. He. Touching. You?" he said again, slowly and deliberately.

"He wasn't..." I shook my head. "He's a coach. He was lifting me up to the bars. That was all. Why? Are you worried I was giving him a blowjob before you got there?"

Apparently that was the wrong thing to say, because Mannix's face turned red. He screeched the SUV down a side street and slammed on the brakes so hard I almost bounced my head on the dashboard.

"What the hell, Mannix?" My head spun for a moment. "Are you trying to kill us?"

Judging by the expression on his face, that was exactly what he was trying to do.

He lurched towards me. I backed up until my shoulders hit the SUV's window. The expression on his face was intense, his eyes darker than ever.

He grabbed a fistful of my hair and curled it around his fingers. He drew me toward him until my face was a couple of centimetres from his. His breath was blazing hot on my cheek.

My heart thundered through my chest. I could hardly think, barely breathe. Being so close to him was an attack on all of my senses. Heat radiated off him, churned with a dose of fury and lust. If I looked down, I knew I'd see his hard cock pressed against the zipper of his jeans. The feel and smell of him was pure sex.

Oh fuck.

"Why did he touch you?" he growled. His teeth were gritted together, bared like a wild animal. If Charlie was here, he might bite his head off with one snap.

"I told you, he's a coach. He was doing his job. Nothing else. It was harmless." I swallowed hard. "Why do you care anyway?"

His fist tightened around my head to the point of pain. "Because no one touches you," he said slowly, his tone menacing, bordering on terrifying. "No one touches you but *me*. Do you understand me? *No one.*"

My head spun harder. What the hell was he saying? I was convinced he hated my guts, but then he said things like that? He was going to give me whiplash with his sudden change.

"I don't—"

He pulled me until his stubble scratched over my lips and the side of my cheek. My eyes watered from the pain, but I didn't want him to stop. Didn't want him to let go.

"Princess, I know you want me as much as I want you. You want me to fuck you until you scream. I see it in your eyes every time you look at me. Did you think I wouldn't notice? Did you think I wouldn't feel it too? The moment I set eyes on you, I knew you were mine. You knew it, too, didn't you? Your pussy is dripping right now. Dripping for me."

I didn't know how to answer that, so I let out a breathless whimper. I was wetter than hell. Yes, I wanted him to touch me, but I still wasn't convinced he didn't hate me. I was also not convinced I'd say no to anything he tried to do to me. Yeah, I wanted him so bad it hurt. I wanted to spread my thighs and let him bury his face between them. I wanted to feel him fill me with every centimetre he had.

"You are mine and no one touches you but me," he said again. "I don't give a fuck if he's a coach or a fucking gynaecologist. No one lays a hand on you. Do you hear me? Do you?"

"Ye— Yes I do," I said, my voice barely above a whisper.

He paused for a moment, then brushed his lips over mine. It was barely a kiss. A feather light touch. And then he released my hair and sat back.

"We should get back," he said like nothing happened. "I have things to do. If you need to go anywhere, I'll drive you. I'll watch the whole time you're there if I have to."

I combed my fingers through my hair to straighten it and sat back up in my seat. "That could make it difficult to teach if you're lurking around all the time." My heart slowed gradually, but my whole body throbbed with need. What would it be like to have him on top of me? Inside me? The thought threatened to consume me like an inferno.

"Don't give me an excuse to lurk around then," he said. As if I was somehow responsible for the actions of someone else.

Okay, I didn't need Charlie's help, but the whole

thing was harmless. Apparently Mannix didn't see it that way.

"I have a feeling you'll lurk anyway," I said.

He cut me a look as he restarted the engine. "I take good care of what's mine. I might even buy you a pretty little pink car with a pink bow, myself."

I believed him.

"I prefer black," I said.

"I think I'll just drive you around myself for a while." He drove the SUV back out into the main road, but just as wild and reckless as before.

"Fine, but maybe don't kill me with your driving," I said. That would really put a dampener on this... whatever this was. I couldn't deny the attraction but could I handle his intensity? Did I want to try?

For some reason I wasn't even sure of myself, I actually did. As well as being hot, Mannix was fascinating. When he wasn't being an asshole, I felt safe from the world around him. Like...if anyone hurt me, he wouldn't hesitate to protect me from and deal with them.

The question was, who would protect me from him?

CHAPTER SEVEN

KENNEDY

I was dreaming but I couldn't get myself to wake up. In my dream, several figures started towards me. Three wore black head coverings like they were executioners. A fourth had no face, but his neck was wide open, gaping and shining with blood.

They shuffled towards me. Their hands were by their sides, but at the same time, they seemed to be reaching for me.

"We'll find you, little mouse. There's nowhere you can run and hide from us. Nowhere we can't find you."

I couldn't tell which one of them was speaking. Maybe it was all of them. The words echoed through my mind like they were on feedback, on a continuous loop. Speaking over each other more and more, becoming louder and louder like a crescendo.

Something pinned my wrists to either side of my face. The figures got closer. I writhed and struggled, but couldn't move. They were going to catch me, and when they did, I was dead. If I let them touch me, I would wither and die or turn into dust.

I couldn't let them touch me. Whatever it took, I had to stop that from happening.

I struggled harder. Tipped back my head and screamed.

And screamed.

"Princess. Princess, come on. I've got you. Shhh." Vice-like hands gripped my wrists, holding me tighter.

My eyes snapped open and I found myself in dim light.

My bedroom.

Mannix lay beside me, his fingers hard around my wrists, his face centimetres from mine.

"There you are." His grip relaxed slightly. "Another nightmare?"

"Another..." I blinked a couple of times, still trying to orient myself.

"You've had them every night since I got here."

He let go of my wrists and propped himself up on his elbow. "This one sounded worse than the others."

Slowly, I managed to register two facts. First, Mannix was in my bed. Second, he'd come in here to help me when I was having a bad dream.

Wait, there was a third fact—he was naked except for a pair of boxer shorts. It went to show how disturbed I was after the nightmare that I didn't notice that straight away.

He brushed hair off my sweaty brow. "You okay?"

"I— Yeah." I wanted to tell him everything. To get the memory of that night off my chest. I didn't know him well enough to know if I could trust him, so I just said, "Thanks."

He grabbed up the water bottle I kept beside my bed and offered it to me. I took a couple of sips and set it back down.

"Better?" He cocked his head at me. He seemed genuinely concerned. Maybe the aloof guy he'd been since he first pulled up with Ice and Ares was an act to protect himself. From what though?

"Much better. I'm sorry if I disturbed your sleep. I guess moving to a new place has me more on edge than I thought." That was lame, but that was all I could come up with right now.

"Dusk Bay has that effect on people." He slipped

a hand under the hem of my singlet and across my stomach. "I'll have to give you something to keep your mind off it."

A shiver went all the way through me and left a pool of heat in my core. His fingers were calloused, rough on my skin, but enticing.

"Mannix..."

His mouth right next to my ear he whispered, "Tell me something, Princess. How many guys have touched you? How many guys have fucked that tight little pussy?" He spoke as though he would track down every last one and trim their cocks off at their balls.

My tongue darted over my lips. I whispered, "None."

His hand stilled and he drew in a breath of surprise. "None? My sweet little Princess is a sweet little virgin?"

"Yeah. I just never... Found someone I wanted to... be with." There were opportunities, but none that excited me the way Mannix, Ares and Ice did. What would Mannix do if either of his friends touched me? It didn't matter in Ares' case, since he obviously hated my guts, but Ice was sweet. How far would Mannix really take it? It was one thing to say no one else could touch me and another to act on it. Especially when the other guy was a close friend.

"Good." He lowered his mouth to mine and kissed me softly.

Just that gentle touch set my body on fire. Strange how a guy who could be so forceful, could also be so sweet. His mouth tasted of mint and some kind of spice.

His tongue slipped between my lips and stroked over my teeth, probing deeper like he wanted to explore every bit of me.

His hand slid up my stomach, to cup my breast. He palmed my nipple until it was rock hard. Then he worked on the other one.

"Tell me how much you want me, Princess," he whispered between kisses. "Tell me you want me to fuck you."

Did I? I mean, yes I did, but this was going so fast.

"I want you to...touch me," I said tentatively.

"Just touch? I can start with that." He peeled up the front of my singlet and moved down to trace circles around my nipple with his tongue. This was already far more than I ever did with anyone else.

"This nipple is mine." He closed his lips around it and sucked, while at the same time teasing me with his tongue. "And so is this one." He switched over to my other nipple. "So tasty."

His touch felt so good. Better than good, it felt right.

He abandoned my nipples and kissed his way slowly down my body. He hooked his thumbs into my panties and ripped them in two.

"I'll buy you new ones." He unapologetically tossed both pieces aside and moved down lower. He parted my thighs with firm, but still gentle fingers.

"Has anyone else licked you down here?" His eyes were intense on mine.

"No, no one."

Was he really about to... I'd thought about this more times than I could count, but when his tongue grazed over my clit, it was so much better than I could have imagined.

He groaned. "Fucking hell, Princess, you taste like pure addictive sin." He lapped at me a couple of times before he added, "This pussy is mine too. Mine to taste." Lick. "Mine to nibble." Lick. "Mine to make come."

I could only moan in response. I was speeding towards an orgasm faster than Mannix's driving. My whole body was on fire, burning like his touch was hot oil on an open flame.

I stiffened when he slipped a finger inside me. It felt strange at first, and more than a bit mindblowing.

He raised his face and said, "Relax, Princess." He slid his finger in and out slowly. "You feel amazing and so fucking wet. This is practice for when you take my cock."

When I finally let myself relax, he slid in another finger. He stroked me inside while his tongue worked the outside.

"Come for me, Princess," he said, his voice muffled by my thighs. "Show me you're mine."

I couldn't have stopped myself if I wanted to. He shattered me into a thousand, breathless, bucking pieces. The world exploded into a prism of light, lost in the sound of thundering blood. With my fingers or a vibrator, I'd never come so hard. Or stayed up in the atmosphere so long.

I finally flopped back onto the mattress. He slipped his fingers out of me and scooted up to press one between my lips.

"See how delicious you taste? My delicious Princess." He held it there while I sucked it clean. The combination of my juices and the salt on his skin were divine.

He lay down beside me and gathered me up in his arms. "I won't fuck you tonight. I want to, but I'll give you a little bit of time to be ready for me. I'll come to you every night and make you come for me. And when you're ready, I'll fuck that tight little pussy. Just like my father is probably fucking your mother right now. When they get married, nothing has to change between us. When I'm your step-brother, you'll still be mine."

He stroked my hair, tangling his fingers in the soft waves.

He whispered in my ear, "Tell me who you belong to."

I swallowed. My voice a little shaky, I said, "You. I belong to you. Soon I'll be ready for your cock." He was right, I needed some time to think about it and process everything. I wanted to feel him inside me, but not tonight. Not yet.

"Of course you will. You're my princess. I'm going to claim you fully. Every beautiful centimetre of your gorgeous body. I'm going to fill you so much you'll overflow, but you'll still beg for more."

"You think I'm gorgeous?" I said sleepily.

He chuckled, low and deep. "You're the most gorgeous woman I've ever seen. The more of you I see, the more I think, I know, every bit of you is abso-lutely fucking beautiful."

My face heated. What? When I looked in the

mirror was a girl with bright red hair, pale skin and a bunch of freckles. I was cute, but I'd never seen myself as beautiful before.

The way he said it almost made me believe it. If he kept saying it, someday I would.

"What will your father say?" If Leo hated the idea of us being together, he could easily kick me out of his house and his son's life, even if it meant upsetting my mother. Leo was the kind of man who got what he wanted. That must run in the family.

"Leave him to me. It won't be a problem."

Why did those words leave me slightly chilled?

"Are you worried your mother will object?" he asked.

"I'm not sure what she'll say," I admitted. She'd want me to be happy, but the situation was all kinds of complicated, especially if things turned bad. On the other hand, it wasn't as though Mannix and I were related by blood. Where was the harm in us making each other feel good? "What will Ares and Ice say?"

"They'll be jealous as fuck," he said, sounding smug. "They both want you too."

"They do? Ares—"

"Ares has his head stuck up his ass," Mannix said. "With good reason, but that's another story. Let's not talk about them anymore. Do you want to talk about the nightmare?"

I shivered. "Not really. I'd prefer to forget about it. Will you stay with me for a while?" With his arms around me, I might sleep without dreaming. If anything could keep the darkness away, it would be his muscles and the comfort of his warm body.

"You couldn't make me leave if you held a gun to my head," he said.

I got the impression he meant that literally. Maybe the reason I thought he could keep the darkness away was because he was part of it. It might curl itself around him so they could comfort each other.

If I thought he was dark, then what did that make me? A girl who lay in the arms of her stepbrother-to-be while his face smelled of me, knowing he wanted to claim every part of me, inside and out.

What would he give me in return? His body, certainly. But what about his heart?

What about mine? A guy like him could tear me apart and walk away, leaving me shattered on the floor. I should guard my heart against him, but part of me didn't want to. A reckless voice inside told me to let go, but I didn't want to jump into freefall without some kind of parachute.

Right now, I didn't even have a scrap of fabric.

CHAPTER EIGHT

KENNEDY

"So," Ice drawled, "what are you studying?" He stood at my shoulder, his breath brushing my neck.

"Computer science," I said without looking away from the screen. I was trying to play it cool, but I hadn't read a word since he entered the kitchen. After what Mannix said about him and Ares wanting me, I was hyper-aware around all three of them. More so than before.

"I'm sure that sounds super geeky." It was a great way of scaring guys off. Too many of them couldn't deal with a smart woman. I couldn't deal with a guy who was threatened by someone with brains.

"I think it sounds super cool." He put his hands on my shoulders and lightly started to massage the knots.

"I was going to ask what you studied but I'm guessing it's massage therapy." I dropped my head forward and let him work, while keeping half an ear out for Mannix and Ares.

Mannix had said something about a problem with one of the cars. Ares went to help him, leaving Ice and I alone. I presumed they were letting the mechanic onto the property, because I doubted these rich boys knew much about engines.

But if Mannix was going to get pissed off about Ice touching me...

Ice chuckled.

My heart skipped a beat and started racing. *It was just a laugh*, I told myself. Why did it get to me so much?

"No, I studied forensic pathology. I'm fascinated about how one part of the human anatomy is attached to another. Like this—" He squeezed my shoulder lightly. "Is attached to this." He traced circles around the top of my chest with the pad of his thumb, brushed across the top of my breast.

"And this—" He slid a finger down my arm and traced circles around the crook of my elbow. "This innocent little crook is an erogenous zone."

It certainly was. I was going to go wild if he kept doing that.

I shivered.

"The whole body is full of interesting muscles and nerve endings," he continued. "A touch here can elicit a reaction there." The heel of his hand slid over my collarbone. My nipples immediately pebbled in response. He moved his hand up and down, slow and light.

"Is that making you wet, Beautiful?"

Without waiting for an answer he moved his hand over to my other collarbone.

I swallowed hard. His touch was like pure electricity on my skin.

"The funny thing is, the body can react without physical stimuli. Sometimes all it takes is words."

He braced himself on the kitchen island, one hand on either side of me, almost but not quite touching me. He whispered in my ear.

"I want to tear off all your clothes, sit you up on the bench top and bury my face between your legs. Then, when you're as wet as hell, I want to impale you on my cock, all the way to my balls. I want to feel your wet heat around me, muscles convulsing. I want to feel the friction as I fuck you slowly, then quickly. I want to feel my balls burst as I come inside you, filling you all the way up."

He breathed hard out his nose. "Did that make you even wetter? It made me hard as fuck."

He adjusted his pants as he stepped away from me. "They say the brain is the sexiest organ in the human body. I think it's incredible because I can arouse you—and myself—but I can also scare you with words."

"I'm sure you could." I knew all too well how terrifying words could be. And he was right, I was wet from both his voice and imagining him doing those things to me.

"What are you doing?"

My eyes snapped up, toward the door.

How long had Mannix been standing there? Ares was right behind him. They both looked pissed.

"Keeping Kennedy company," Ice said lightly. "I think we need to talk, the four of us. There's something very much in the air that needs to be cleared." If he noticed the glares they both gave him, he showed no sign. He wasn't intimidated by them one bit.

That made one of us.

Mannix stepped up behind me and placed his hands on my shoulders. A gesture of pure possessiveness. Could he see the blush on my cheeks? Surely he must have noticed my reaction to Ice's words and touch? The touch was innocent. Ish. The words? Definitely not.

"What the fuck are you talking about?" Ares demanded.

Ice stepped around to the other side of the island and nodded at me. "I'm talking about Kennedy."

The air was thick with testosterone. I could almost smell it.

"She's mine," Mannix growled.

"I think she should be ours," Ice said reasonably. He could have been talking about last night's soup, or the rising cost of eggs.

"You've gone fucking soft in the head or the cock," Ares snarled.

Ice looked at him like he'd asked him what his favourite colour was. "My head and cock are as hard as ever." He looked back to Mannix. "We share everything, why not her?"

"You guys are out of your fucking mind." Ares muttered something to himself about people thinking with their cock before he stalked out of the room.

I might be out of my mind too, because I was wondering what it would be like to be sandwiched between Ice and Mannix.

Ice shrugged. "Don't you think it should be up to Kennedy to decide?"

I was wondering when one of them might remember I should have a say in this.

Mannix's fingers tightened convulsively, digging into the bones of my shoulders.

"Princess..." He was obviously not used to asking for other people's opinions, or for permission. Although, he respected my choice not to fuck him last night when I wasn't ready, so maybe there was room for him to respect my other choices.

"I like you both," I said slowly and carefully. "I don't want to come between you." I didn't realise my inadvertent innuendo until Ice grinned.

I snorted softly. "Okay, I sort of do, some day. But I don't want you to fight over me. I don't want to mess up your friendship with each other or with Ares. I'll move out of it becomes a—"

"No," Mannix said quickly and with force. "No moving out." He was silent for a while and I could almost see him chewing his thoughts and trying hard not to spit them out.

"You both want this?" he asked finally. "You two and me? Ares too if he stops getting his dick in a knot?"

I looked at him over my shoulder. "What do you want?"

He regarded me intently. "I want you. If it means

sharing you with guys I think of as my brothers, then so fucking be it."

"You can fuck me too if you want." Ice grinned.

I expected Mannix to deny wanting to do anything like that, but he didn't. He gave Ice a long look and then returned his gaze to me.

"It's agreed then. One of us will be the first to fuck you. When the time is right."

I glanced over to Ice, who nodded.

"Works for me. As long as I get my turn." He gave me a look that made me even wetter than any of his words had.

At this rate, I was going to leave puddles behind wherever I went. I could hardly believe we were casually discussing me dating all three of them. Screwing all three of them. I was turned on enough to let them bend me over the kitchen table and fuck me here and now.

"One condition," Mannix said. "No one touches her but us. Not that dickhead coach, no one."

"I can agree with that." Ice opened a drawer and pulled out a large knife. "I know just what to do with them if they overstep." He drew a precise line in the air, then peeled it back with his fingertips as though opening a chest cavity. He reached in and curled his fingers around an imaginary heart. He pulled his hand back and cocked his head, pretending real blood dripped from his fingers.

"I know how to make it look like an accident." Ice tossed the imaginary heart over his shoulder.

I pictured it hitting the wall and sliding down, leaving a smear of blood behind it.

"Why bother?" Mannix shrugged. "We could leave it as a warning."

Was it wrong that I found all of this incredibly hot? Fucked up, but hot. I mean, it wasn't like they'd actually act on it.

Would they?

"I guess I belong to both of you then," I said softly.

Ice, who was swishing the knife around in the air, froze and smiled. "I like the sound of that. Our girl. Our *smart* girl," he added.

He glanced at Mannix. "I bet your father can think of a hundred ways to put a computer science major to good use."

Mannix grunted. "Probably, but let's not get ahead of ourselves."

I wanted to ask him why, but he gripped my chin, turned my face toward him and kissed me.

Ice, with the knife still in his hand, skipped

around the island, turned my face the other way and kissed me too, all teeth, tongue and stubble.

In the corner of my eye, I saw the knife near my shoulder, a hair or two from my ear.

Like the knife was that night in the forest. Right before it was pulled across the man's throat. The gush of blood... The gurgle...

I gasped involuntarily.

"Figures you'd be a shit kisser," Mannix told him.

"No it's just—" I leaned away from the knife. "It's just *that*."

Instead of taking it away, Ice trailed the tip of the knife down my cheek, slow and careful. It tickled slightly. My heart raced as the light glanced off it. One slip of his hand and he'd slice my cheek open.

"I would never hurt you," he said softly. "This is just a tool. Sometimes used for bad, but mostly just to cut onions." He took the blade away and made a series of tiny dicing gestures in the air. "Occasionally steak." His dicing became a cut of what looked like very well cooked beef.

"Knives don't hurt people, people hurt people?" I didn't take my eyes off the blade. I put a hand to my cheek, but I knew he hadn't broken the skin.

"Exactly. And sometimes people hurt them-selves," Mannix said. "But if anyone tries to touch you, they will end up resembling an onion. I've seen the way Ice works, he could do it too."

I believed him.

"I wanted to be a doctor." Ice held the blade up in front of his face as though fascinated by the stainless steel. "A surgeon. But I decided autopsies would be more interesting than surgery."

"Fewer malpractice suits from dead people," Mannix said dryly.

Ice grinned, his smile eerily cut in two by the blade. "Yep."

"What did you study?" I asked Mannix. Partly because I wanted to know and partly to change the subject and stop looking at the knife.

He shrugged one shoulder. "Business. Someone has to step into Dad's shoes."

I had a feeling there was more to it than that, but he didn't seem to want to elaborate. I didn't ask. If there was more, he'd tell me when he was ready.

"What did Ares study?" Apart from the inside of his own asshole.

"Believe it or not, psychology," Ice said. "I'll leave it to you to ask him why."

Considering he wouldn't give me the time of day, I doubted he'd give me an answer to anything that might vaguely resemble a personal question.

It was difficult to see how I could avoid making waves between the three guys, but if they wanted to try, then I would. As long as knives were kept for cutting food and not people. Especially me. I believed them when they said they wouldn't hurt me. I also believed them when they said they'd hurt anyone who touched me when they shouldn't. At some point, maybe I could confide in them about what I saw that night. If anyone could keep me safe from three crazy masked murderers, then these guys could.

Right?

"Did someone mention skinny-dipping later tonight?" Ice said innocently.

No one had, but the idea sent a thrill of excitement through me. Naked in a pool with two, maybe three hot guys. Dusk Bay might not be so bad after all.

CHAPTER NINE

MANNIX

"You're out of your fucking mind," Ares snarled. His blue eyes were dark and narrowed, razor-sharp glare directed straight at me. "You two are going to share a woman, and think I should too?"

I shrugged and sipped my beer. "Kennedy isn't just any woman."

"No, she's your step sister."

"Not yet she's not." I hooked my ankle around another pool chair and dragged it over so I could put my feet on it. "Who cares anyway? She's smoking hot, smart and her pussy tastes better than this beer." I held up the bottle for a moment before taking another long sip.

Ares groaned. "You know how her pussy tastes?" He shook his head. "I should have known you'd fucked her already. How long did it take you? An hour?"

"I didn't say I fucked her," I said. "We didn't get to that. Not yet. But we will." Soon. I didn't want to rush her into anything she wasn't ready for, but I wouldn't wait too long. My cock ached thinking about her.

"What, is she a virgin or something?" Ares laughed. He stopped when he saw my expression. "Really?" Now he looked interested. "I didn't know there were any of those left in Australia. In Victoria, anyway."

"That explains the vibe I got from her," Ice said thoughtfully. "Naïve, innocent and sweet. Three of my favourite things."

"You could be describing me," I joked. They both laughed. I was the exact opposite of innocent and naïve. We all were.

"So, you need help corrupting this girl?" Ares asked. "Moving to Dusk Bay would do that sooner or later, without my help."

"I don't want her corrupted," I said firmly. I sighed into my beer bottle. "Sooner or later she has to know who we are, what we are and what we do."

"The Devils of Dusk Bay," Ice said softly. "Wasn't that what your father wanted us to be?"

"Haven't we lived up to it yet?" I raised my eyebrows at him.

"I think we have a way to go." Ice sipped his beer. "Our reputation is growing, but there's always room for more."

"You won't be happy until people are pissing themselves at the idea of us," Ares told him.

"Isn't that what you want too?" Ice asked. "I'm just happy if I get to do a little carving once in a while."

"Once in a while being at least once a day," I told him. Ares and I liked to take care of business, whatever that meant at the time. Ice, he seemed to be in it for the bloodshed. I once saw him torture a man for three days, for the fun and fascination of it. He claimed he wanted to see how long the man would last with no tongue and in constant agony. He got off on it.

I've known him all my life, long enough that I got him, for the most part. He was harmless unless you were the wrong person. I basically made my life's work not to be the wrong person.

"And you think someone sweet, innocent and naïve isn't going to freak the fuck out when she finds out who we are?" Ares asked.

"She might be sweet, but she's not stupid," I

said. "She has to know the kind of people my father and her mother are, even if it's deep down. Sooner or later, she'll face the truth and we'll help her through it. She belongs to us and *with* us. She'll be fine." She had to be, because if she wasn't, then she'd be one of the wrong people. I couldn't guess how long Ice would keep her alive to listen to her pretty screams. I suspected it would be days at least.

"You seem very sure of that," Ares said. "What happens if we tell her and she turns on us? Do you have the balls to do what needs to be done?"

"I have balls of iron," I said coldly. They were constantly hard around my Princess. Aching to release into her gorgeous body. I wished she was here with us right now for me to do just that. Last time I saw her, she was in her bedroom, studying. After a long day of teaching gymnastics to a room full of brats, I decided to leave her to it. As long as I knew exactly where she was, I could give her a bit of space.

"Is that why you're reluctant to get involved with her?" I asked Ares. "Are you worried she'll make you soft?" I was goading him on purpose. Ares wouldn't turn soft for a puppy, much less a woman. But this arrangement only worked if everyone agreed.

"Fuck off," Ares snarled. "Do you want me

involved with your girlfriend so you can see my cock once in a while?"

"I've seen your cock plenty of times," I said. "It's nothing special. Not as big and thick as mine."

He flipped me off. "That's bullshit and you know it."

I shrugged. "Keep telling yourself that. The point is, we hang out together all the time. If Kennedy is going out with all of us and fucking all of us, then we don't have to worry about any bros before hos shit." The three of us were a tight unit. The last thing we needed was three other people breaking that up.

"I'll think about it," Ares said. "I'm not saying I wouldn't rail her in a heartbeat, but I don't know if I want to share with you fuckers. I've never been big on taking turns. I might just hunt down my own pussy. You dickheads aren't going to let her get in the way, are you? Posse before pussy, like we agreed."

"She won't get in the way," I assured him. He was a stubborn prick sometimes. He'd come around eventually, but if he didn't, then whatever. More holes for Ice and I.

"She can be part of our posse," Ice said. "The Devils and the Beautiful. She could be the Beautiful Devil."

I preferred my nickname for her, but I didn't

bother to mention it. We didn't have to share every single thing.

"Are you listening to yourselves?" Ares asked. "What guarantee do you have that she'd want anything to do with any of us when she knows what we're really like? You say she'll be fine, but what if she's not? Can you really imagine her with blood on her hands?"

"She doesn't have to have blood on her hands," I argued. "She's learning how to prevent people from hacking systems like my father's. She could be useful for that. I bet anything she knows how to hack into those systems too. Imagine how much fun we could have, fucking with the Bell family bank accounts." She could probably make herself a billionaire with a few keystrokes. That would be all kinds of awesome.

"Is your psychology degree telling you sweet, innocent people will only ever be that?" I asked. "Because I know it's not. Even people who think they're decent are really assholes deep down."

"It's not even deep down for some people," Ares said pointedly.

I grinned unashamedly. I gave up trying to be nice a long time ago. Around at the same time I noticed Ares seemed to have more fun being his honest, nasty self. The only one of us who even tried was Ice, but I always suspected that was an act to gain people's trust. He was the only one of us people would turn their backs on. Ironically, he was the one they should never look away from, if they preferred their internal organs inside their bodies.

Ares and I killed when we needed to, but Ice did it for fun. For shits and giggles. These days, we tended to leave most of the killing to him. He'd complain if we didn't.

"I feel like you have the rest of your life planned out, with your stepsister right in the middle of it," Ares said slowly.

"What's wrong with that?" I asked. "I'm going to take over my father's business and she'll be by my side. That's where she belongs. The three of us and her. Think how powerful we'll be. We might even be powerful enough to challenge Caleb Brantley some day. Or Reuben Brantley." The thought gave me a chill up and down my spine. The idea of that much power made my cock hard. We would be above any law, anywhere. We could do whatever we wanted to whoever we wanted and no one would dare stand against us.

"Don't say that too fucking loud," Ares warned. "The walls might have ears here too." He gestured around the dark pool area. The only lights were the handful under the water, and those inside the house.

"If they do, I'll deal with them." If I had to take out my father or my older brother, Gunnar, to keep my two other brothers safe, then that's what I'd do. Ice would have fun dissecting Leonardo Cassani, in spite of the fact my father let him get away with a lot of things others wouldn't. Ice was only loyal to him up to a point. Once he was off his leash, he'd go wild. Figuratively speaking. Ice's version of wild was understated and methodical. And very bloody.

"How are you going to deal when Reuben Brantley sends an assassin after you?" Ares asked.

"He won't," I said with certainty. "As far as anyone knows, we're loyal to the people we're supposed to be loyal to. We'll keep doing that as long as it covers our asses. Whatever it takes for us to survive and thrive." At the end of the day, that was all that mattered. There was nothing I wouldn't do to ensure that. No one I wouldn't step on, step over or kill. Whatever I had to do, I'd do it.

"Has it crossed your mind that your precious stepsister and her mother might be working for someone who doesn't have our interests at heart?" Ares asked. "You're so sure she's sweet and innocent, but what if she works for the Bell family? Or is one of them? She's only a year or two older than Chloe and Lila Bell. They could be best friends for all you know."

"You think I'd let someone like Helen Knight into my home without a very thorough background check?" I asked coolly. Who did he think he was talking to? I sure as fuck wasn't born yesterday. No one crossed the threshold without me knowing exactly who they were and why they were here. I made sure of that.

"Who would have the skills to make a background check come up exactly the way they wanted?" Ares asked thoughtfully. "Oh, I know. A computer science major. Just because her file says she's a twenty-one-year-old university student who does gymnastics in her spare time, doesn't mean she's not really a thirty-one-year-old spy for another mob family."

I snorted. "She's definitely not thirty-one." He planted a seed of doubt in my mind though. He was right in saying Kennedy could have changed the information with a few clicks. On the other hand, we had people working for us who had the skills she was just learning. If anything was changed, chances are they would have found it.

If it was there to be found. I knew as well as

anyone that meetings often took place face-to-face, but there would be some record of that, somewhere. On her phone perhaps? I'd take a look later. I wanted to make sure she wasn't talking to any other guys anyway, or letting them talk to her. If she was, I'd let Ice take care of them.

Speaking of Ice, where the fuck was he?

I glanced around, but he was nowhere to be seen. In a flash of realisation, I knew where he'd gone and why.

"Motherfucker."

CHAPTER TEN

KENNEDY

I pinched the bridge of my nose and squeezed my eyes shut. I'd spent way too long staring at this report. The words on the screen were starting to blur together.

Just a bit longer, I told myself.

I glanced at the time in the bottom corner of the screen. It was close to midnight. Early for me, but not after a long day of coaching. Nicola offered me a job as Charlie suggested she would, but then I ended up covering for him when he got sick. Food poisoning, apparently. Hopefully that was all.

I hadn't forgotten how Mannix got all pissy about him touching me. It was completely innocent, but I knew Mannix saw it differently. If the tables were turned and he was the one lifting a woman up to the uneven bars, I might be jealous too.

Or if Ice did it.

Okay, Ares too. He was a free agent and could do what he wanted, but I couldn't help thinking of him as mine, if only a little bit.

I blinked and tried to focus on the screen.

"All work and no play..." Ice whispered as he silently pushed my door open.

"Hey." Once, I would have been annoyed at the interruption, but today I was glad for the chance to take a break. I closed my screen and put my laptop on the table beside my bed.

"Are the other guys with you?" I leaned over to look past him, but the corridor was dark and empty.

"Nope, I snuck away when they were having a deep and meaningful conversation about cock size." Ice grinned and stepped into the room. He shut the door behind him.

"Who would win that argument?" The skinny dipping hadn't happened yet so all I had to go on was my imagination. Which I admit was very fertile. When I wasn't having nightmares, I was dreaming and fantasising about all three guys. Fantasies that left me wet and panting, and tracing circles around my clit with my fingertips.

The bed dipped as Ice sat down beside me.

"Ares," he said. "Although, Mannix and I give him a run for his money. He just happens to be thicker than us. Mannix is a bit longer. Mine slants to the left a little, but has the added bonus of some jewellery."

My eyes widened. "Jewellery?" My mouth was suddenly dry.

"You want to see?" His hands hovered over the button of his jeans. His eyebrows were raised and he looked straight at me. Not pressuring, not being sleazy, just happy to share.

"Um." Great, now I looked like a complete idiot. I'd never been ashamed of being a virgin, but the only cocks I ever saw were on the Internet. Unless you counted the shared bathrooms in preschool, which I didn't.

He placed his hands on the top of the bed covers behind him and leaned back.

"I didn't mean to make you uncomfortable. I'm sorry if I did."

I licked my lips. "You didn't. I've just been thinking a lot about..." If my face was any hotter I'd catch fire.

"External and internal stimuli?" he asked.

"Right, that." I hadn't been able to think of much

else, even with the gymnastics class and the report I was supposed to write. I felt like my senses were full of the smell and feel of Mannix and Ice.

"Would you like some more?" he asked softly.

I swallowed hard.

"Yes, please," I whispered.

He slowly raised one hand as though I was a wild animal, and cupped my cheek. He stroked the pad of his thumb across my jawline and leaned in to brush his lips over mine.

Gradually, his touch became firmer, kisses more demanding. He swiped his tongue across my lips and into my mouth.

Before I lost my breath completely, he drew back.

His hand still on my cheek, he said, "Close your eyes."

My heart raced, but I shut them.

"Imagine me sliding my hands up under your shirt. Across the tight, smooth skin of your stomach. Up to the bottom of your breasts."

As he spoke, I could almost feel him doing those things. He wasn't. The only place he touched me was my cheek. His voice was so hypnotic, so enticing, he gave me tingles everywhere.

"Imagine my fingers circling your nipples. You

know how that feels, don't you? You've touched yourself?"

"Yes," I whispered.

"Good," he said softly. "Imagine me rolling those stiff little peaks between my thumb and forefinger. They feel so perfect."

I didn't open my eyes, but I knew he had his closed too, imagining the same thing.

"Picture my mouth around one of your nipples. Sucking like a baby trying to get milk. Then sucking the other one. At the same time, my hands slide off your panties. You take off my pants until we're lying side by side, naked. I take your hand and guide it down to my cock. You curl your fingers around my length, stroking and teasing. You position me outside your pussy. You're wet. So wet. I slide inside you. All the way in, nice and deep."

I groaned. "Please..." I wasn't exactly sure what I was asking for, but I needed to feel, not just imagine.

"Please what?" he asked, his mouth right near my ear. "Tell me what you need."

"I need..." I hesitated. "I need it to be real. I want you to..." I could barely think straight, much less put the thoughts into coherent words.

His next words were so faint, I almost didn't hear them.

"Fuck you?"

My body trembled. Was that what I wanted? Did I need to take more time to think about it? I knew he'd respect me if I did, but I didn't. I wanted this. I wanted him.

No louder than he had spoken I said, "Yes."

The word barely left my lips before his hands gripped the hem of my shirt and he was pulling it over my head. I took off my bra hours ago, so my chest was bare, nipples as hard as blush coloured rocks.

"I thought your breasts would be beautiful," he said, sounding reverent. "But they're even more incredible than I imagined." His tone was still hypnotic, but he did all the things he said he would, first with his hands and then with his mouth.

When I was panting and ready to beg for more, he pushed me back gently until I lay on top of the covers. He hooked his fingers into my panties and tugged them off.

Then, not without a flourish, he undid his jeans and pushed them down.

I stared.

The tip of his cock was decorated with two long bars which crossed over each other, a ball at all four points like a compass. Like he'd said, his cock pointed north-west, towards me but with a slant.

"What is..." I pointed tentatively.

He glanced down. "It's called a magic cross." He gripped my finger between his thumb and forefinger and brought it all the way until it touched his cock. He was hot and hard. Gently, giving me time to pull away, he guided me until my fingers were all the way around his length.

"Have you ever touched a cock before?" he asked.

My tongue darted over my lips and I shook my head. "Never. It feels— thick."

His laugh was soft and deep in the back of his throat. "Thank you. I don't mind my cock being described as thick." He pried my thighs open with his hands and let them explore the insides of my legs and up to my pussy.

He took his time with every movement. Every stroke. Every circle. When he slid his fingers inside me, he did it with care, like he didn't want to hurt me.

When I came against his fingers, he smiled. The orgasm he drew out of me was like a cascade of fireworks, stars and heated blood. I was so wet I must have coated his hand with my release. Judging by the way he sucked his fingers when he took them away from me, he didn't mind. In fact, it seemed like he was having a tasty snack.

"You make the most beautiful sounds when you come. I look forward to hearing them many, many times."

He was equally careful when he knelt between my knees and positioned his cock outside my entrance.

"Beautiful girl, Mannix said you were a virgin."

"Yes," I whispered. Was Mannix going to be pissed I let Ice be the first? He might be, but I didn't want to stop now. I was ready for this. Wanted it. Did it bother Ice that I was so inexperienced? He didn't seem concerned. If anything he seemed pleased, like he wanted to be my first. That was such a guy thing I would never understand. This was too much thinking right now. I let it all go. All that mattered right now was the moment.

"Perfect," Ice said. "I want you to look at me. Watch me while I slide into you. I want you to watch me take your virginity. I'm going to watch you give it to me. Giving it to me so generously."

I locked my eyes on his and felt him press himself into me. At first, it was just a little bit, just his pierced tip. He waited until I relaxed, then pressed in a little further. Then further. And further until he was all the way inside my body.

It felt strange, but wonderful. So full. I couldn't believe I'd waited so long for this. And yet, I waited just long enough.

"Fuck," he said softly. "You're so incredibly tight. You feel amazing around me. Like you were made to take me inside you."

He started to move, slowly at first, then gradually faster, but always meticulous and careful. Never once did he lose control.

"Would you like to try being on top?" he asked.

"I'm not sure how," I admitted.

He smiled and rolled us over until I knelt on him, his cock still deep inside me. He placed his hands on my hips and helped me rise and fall until I got the rhythm. It wasn't until a couple of bounces that I realised if I angled myself, I could rub my clit on him. I did that a few times before he worked his fingers in between us and rubbed me himself.

"Simultaneous orgasm is difficult to achieve, especially the first time, but it's worth a try." He smiled up at me.

"No pressure," I said. I read about people coming at the same time, but it always seemed so difficult. Like trying to sneeze simultaneously.

His smile widened. "None at all. I just want you to enjoy yourself. I am. It's not going to take me long before I come inside your beautiful body."

For some reason, his words got me going more than ever. That and his touch, and the way his piercings touched me inside.

External and internal stimuli. He knew what he was doing with both of those things.

"I'm close," he whispered, his eyes half closed.

"Me too," I said. "I—" I groaned as I came for the second time. This time so intense I arched my back and rubbed my clit against his fingers with something close to desperation.

We didn't come at the same time. He was at least two or three minutes behind me, thrusting up into me before he stilled and groaned loudly.

"God, Beautiful. Fuck, fuck, fuck, yeah. You're amazing. Absolutely perfect. Your body is ahhh... So good."

I slumped over him. He flopped down to the mattress just as the door flew open.

CHAPTER ELEVEN

KENNEDY

"The fuck, bro?"

Mannix stood silhouetted in the doorway, Ares a few steps behind him.

"Hey," Ice said easily. Hands still on my hips, he eased me off him with a wet plop and tucked me in down behind him. He placed his hands behind his head and crossed his legs at his knees. He looked perfectly comfortable being fully naked in front of them.

"We're just hanging out, right, Beautiful?"

"Um. Right." The blood still pounded through my body and hadn't quite returned to my brain yet. Between that, the guys' sudden appearance and trying to get my head around having had sex for the first time, I was lost for words.

We didn't do anything wrong, but would Mannix and Ares see it that way?

They were both looking at me hungrily and with twin erections.

"Was that what you wanted, Princess?" Mannix's voice was tight, his eyes on Ice before they flickered over to me.

For a moment, I thought Ice would answer for me, but he turned his face to look at me.

My face slightly hot, I sat up and raised my chin. "Yes, it was. It was what I wanted." I wasn't going to apologise for it, even if Mannix was mad at not being my first.

Mannix nodded, then said to Ice, "You're a sneaky prick. We were in the middle of a conversation and you sneak off to fuck our girl."

Ice crossed his legs the other way. "Sometimes you have to seize the moment when it arises. You two can compare cock size all day if you want. I'm going to use mine for what it's intended for. Fucking."

I remembered what he said about the other guys, and looked speculatively at their groins.

"Can you guys shut the door on your way out?" Ice asked.

"Who said we're leaving?" Mannix stepped all

the way into the room. "We just got here. Right, Ares?"

Ares hesitated. "It's getting late. I should get home before my father starts wondering where the fuck I got to." He backed away.

Mannix shrugged. "Suit yourself." When Ares disappeared, followed by the sound of his footsteps heading down the stairs, Mannix closed the door and stepped over to the bed.

"So you two got to have fun. Which one of you is going to suck my cock?" His hands went to the button of his jeans.

I drew in a shaky breath. What would it be like to close my lips around his tip? To slide my tongue across his seem and taste his pre-cum? To feel him thrust in and out of my mouth? Was I ready for that?

Before I could answer, Ice sat up and said, "I will."

Now my heart was really hammering. I wasn't the only woman in the world who got aroused by watching, or reading about two men being intimate, but to see it in person?

Yes please.

Mannix only hesitated for a moment longer before he undid his jeans and pushed them down his hips. His erection jumped free. Ice was right, he was longer. He also had a piercing, but only a single ring at the tip of his cock.

He stepped over and pressed his cock between Ice's eager lips.

My eyes wide, I watched Ice lick his way up and down Mannix's length, from his tip to his balls. Up one side and down the other, then down and back up again. He took him all the way into his mouth and started to suck. The sound and sight turned me on all over again.

"Touch yourself," Mannix said. His eyes went from the guy on his cock, to me. "I know you want to."

"I—" My tongue darted over my lips.

"Touch yourself," he said again, more firmly this time, like he expected to be obeyed.

"Okay." I lay back against the pillows and put my hands between my legs. The entrance to my pussy was sticky with Ice's cum, but I found my clit and started to rub circles around and over it with my fingertips and nails.

"Good girl," Mannix said. "Play with your nipple."

I slowly slid my other hand over my stomach and pinched my nipple. My eyes fluttered shut.

"Open your eyes," Mannix said. "I want you to

watch what Ice is doing to me. Watch me fuck his mouth like someday I'm going to fuck yours."

He rolled his hips slowly, pushing himself deeper into Ice's mouth. He groaned. "Bro, your mouth is all kinds of fucking incredible."

Ice chuckled, but didn't stop sucking.

Watching them together turned me on so hard I was close to coming within a minute or two.

"You two are so fucking hot," Mannix whispered. He thrust harder and faster.

Ice took every movement and rolled with it, even when Mannix was so deep I thought he might gag. I didn't think they'd done this before, but I suspected Ice had thought about it. Both of them had.

Without thinking, I said, "Can you come in his mouth?" Where the hell did that come from? Oh, right, reading romance novels. Where else?

Mannix groaned. "That's my girl. *Our* girl. I *will* come in his mouth for you. What do you want him to do with my cum?"

I considered suggesting Ice spit it out, but I didn't think that was what any of us wanted.

"Swallow it," I said softly. I was right on the edge right now. The sound of Ice's mouth sucking was driving me wilder than wild.

"You heard her," Mannix said breathlessly. He

grunted like a wild animal. His hips stilled as he came.

Ice slid his lips off Mannix's length and turned his face to look at me. The corners of his mouth tipped up in a smile before he swallowed, then licked his lips.

That threw me over the edge into a third, mind and earth-shattering orgasm. My whole body rocked against my fingers, the whole world disappearing except the faces of both guys who watched me intently while I came.

My back arched and I cried out. I bit my lip to keep from screaming.

This house was big, but I didn't need my mother to hear what I was doing. Thankfully, her and Leo's bedroom was right at the other end, so I could have shouted at the top of my lungs and probably not been heard. Still, I didn't want to be too loud.

Mannix stepped out of his jeans and walked around the bed to lie down on the other side of me.

Both guys snuggled into me and somehow managed to get the covers over the top of us.

"That was awesome," Mannix said, sounding sleepy.

"Can I ask you something?" I asked, addressing the question to both of them.

"Anything," Ice said. "I'm an open book as well as an open mouth."

He knew just the right words to say to make my heart race and my mind picture them together again. That would be an instant replay in my brain for a long time. Potentially forever.

"Have you two ever... Done that before?"

"No," Mannix said.

"I've thought about it plenty of times." Ice rolled me onto my side and rested his hand on my ass. "We've talked about it, but we've never acted on it."

"Except the time we shared a kiss," Mannix said.

"Right. But we never talked about it." Ice sounded regretful. "I thought maybe Mannix regretted it." He picked up his head and looked over me and to the other guy.

"No, I never regretted it," Mannix said. "I was worried it would change our relationship too much. But seeing you like this tonight, with our Princess, and willing to suck me off, I wasn't gonna say no."

"Neither was I," Ice said. "I was starting to think you'd never ask. I can't tell you how many times I thought about getting my lips around that cock of yours."

"Would you go further with each other?" I asked tentatively. I already changed their relationship but neither seemed to mind. That didn't mean they wanted to do more than they already had. I could picture it though, and if the sight was as hot as the mental image, then it was definitely something I wanted to see. And hear.

Mannix ran the back of his knuckles down my cheek. "Do you want us to, Princess?"

"I only want you to do what you want to do," I said carefully.

He chuckled. "That wasn't what I was asking. That goes without saying. I want to know if you want to watch us fuck?"

I cleared my throat. "If you do it, and want me to watch..." When he narrowed his eyes I changed my wording. "I'd like to watch."

"Then, if we fuck, you can watch," Mannix said. "There's nothing wrong with asking for what you want. It's the best way to get what you want. If you want either of us, or Ares, tell us. The same way I tell you what I want. It saves a lot of time and bullshit."

"I want a new black hatchback with a bright red ribbon," I said half joking. "Make that a black ribbon."

"Consider it done." Mannix nodded like it was no big deal.

"You don't have to do that," I said with a small laugh.

"How else do we fulfill your dreams?" Ice asked. "If you tell us what you want, we'll make it happen. That's what we do. We make things happen."

Why did that send chills through my body?

"Yes, we do," Mannix agreed. "We'll give you everything you ever wanted and more."

"More than you ever dreamt of," Ice agreed.

"More than any Princess ever had." Mannix dragged his knuckles over my lips and down the line of my jaw. "You'll learn that belonging to us has lots of benefits. No one will dare fuck with you, like they don't dare fuck with us. We'll make sure you're protected wherever you go and whatever you do. We look after what is ours."

"Yes, we do. We all look after each other." Ice squeezed my ass. "Including Ares. Don't worry about him, he'll come around. He needs us, we need him and he wants you too much to walk away."

"I hope he does," I said. "I feel like there's a piece of the puzzle missing." I also didn't want him to stomp off every time he saw me. He spent so much time here, he might as well live here too. The last thing I wanted was for him, for any of them, to feel uncomfortable here.

"That's exactly how I feel too," Ice said. "I thought we had everything figured out, but we didn't. Now we've met you, I know how this is supposed to go. The four of us against the world." He slid the tip of his finger down my ass crack.

I shivered deliciously. Could I keep up with two guys, much less three? Even knowing how inexperienced I was, they all still wanted me. And each other. I could very easily fall into this warm, tight web they wove around me, and I wasn't sure I'd mind. One thing I knew for sure, once I got in, it might be difficult to get back out again. Maybe even impossible.

I wasn't sure how I felt about that, but right now I was safe, held between two smoking hot guys. Guys who seemed to care about me as much as I was coming to care about them.

If this was a trap, maybe I'd jump in feet first and never look back.

CHAPTER TWELVE

KENNEDY

"Nice wheels." Charlie looked sideways at the shiny new Porsche Taycan. The long black ribbon was gone, but the car was still ridiculously incredible and undoubtedly expensive.

I couldn't bring myself to look at how much it was worth. At a guess, I'd say more than a small house in a rural town, and less than a luxury apartment in Sydney or Melbourne. As presents went, it was extravagant. None of the guys would let me refuse it, although Ares muttered something about me spreading my legs for it. When I left for work, Mannix and Ice were busy growling at him for saying that.

"Uh, yeah." How did I begin to explain how I came to have a car like this? "It belongs to my mother." I hated to lie, but the truth was hard for me to believe, much less explain, to someone I barely knew.

"Are you feeling better?" I asked. When he looked confused, I added, "Nicola said you had food poisoning?"

"Oh, right. Food poisoning. Yeah that was... You know, rough. Don't eat chicken that isn't cooked properly." He didn't meet my eye as he spoke. He quickly turned to unlock the gym door and stepped aside to let me enter.

"So that guy the other day, he's a friend of yours?" He followed me in but skirted around me to walk to the office. I had a feeling if he could cross to the other side of the street, he'd do that. What the hell was going on? He'd seemed friendly up until now.

"Mannix? Yeah, I guess you could say we're friends. My mother is marrying his father. We live in the same house." He told me I belonged to him, but we hadn't talked about being boyfriend and girl-friend, or anything official.

Just because he bought me an insanely expensive car didn't mean I'd assume he saw our relationship the same way I did.

"Right." Charlie placed his bag under the desk and sat in the chair to pull off his shoes. "So he's...family?"

"I suppose you could say that." I put my bag beside his and leaned against the desk to take off my own sneakers.

Charlie flinched and turned the chair away from me.

What the hell?

"Are you okay?" I asked. "You seem really... I don't know, on edge. Did I do something to upset you?" I hadn't had enough to do with him to have pissed him off too much, had I?

Some people *were* touchier than others. Mannix and Ares, to name two.

"No," Charlie said quickly. Too quickly. Like he was worried about upsetting me. His eyes flicked to the door and he looked nervous.

"If you're worried about Mannix suddenly coming in like the other day, he's working," I said.

Charlie relaxed visibly, but only slightly. His body was still wound tighter than a corkscrew.

I frowned at him as I tossed my shoes down beside my bag. "Did something—"

The gym door opened and the flood of children began. Charlie looked relieved to have been interrupted and hurried away to gather his class to one side of the gym.

My class consisted of a group of six five-year-old

girls, who would all start school in a few months. Right now, their skills consisted of bouncing, running and some basic tumbling. One of them might be a future champion. Right now, they had crazy short attention spans. It took all my energy and attention to keep them from wandering off or chatting amongst themselves too much.

I kept half an eye on Charlie during the class. He had a group of four boys the same age as the girls. Since boys used different apparatuses, their gymnastic skills were different from the girls. They could often learn together, but where possible they tended to be separated. At least two of them seemed more interested in running up and down the mats than in learning anything. That was one way to work off excess energy. They must be exhausted when they got home. I knew I was.

Charlie didn't say a word to me when the class finished and the next one started.

This was a group of younger children and their parents. My job was mostly to guide the parents while the kids walked over beams a finger width off the floor. Most of the kids looked less interested than the energetic boys, but the parents seemed to have fun.

Charlie disappeared into the office during the

class and closed the door. Maybe I misjudged him the first time we met. He seemed nice and friendly then. Now, he didn't seem to want to know me. I wasn't necessarily here to make friends. I was here to make money. But it wouldn't hurt if he was nice to me. Would it?

"That's it for today, thanks for coming." I stood by the door and waved each parent and child out until they were all gone, then closed it behind the last of them and stepped into the office.

"Break time until the after-school crowd gets here," I remarked.

Charlie grunted. He was bent over the desk, eyes on the computer screen.

I watched his back for a moment, then crouched to feel around in my bag for my lunch. When I stood up again, he hadn't moved. For some reason, that annoyed me.

"Did I do something wrong?" I asked.

I remembered what Mannix said about asking for what I wanted. What I wanted right now was a straight answer. Was that too much to ask?

I thought he wasn't going to respond, until he sat back from the screen and half turned his face towards me. "It's nothing, I'm busy. These invoices won't send themselves."

I perched on the side of the desk beside him. "I could help."

He glanced at my legs, bare up to the hem of my shorts. "No," he said a bit more forcefully than was necessary. "I mean, I'm fine. Nicola or I would need to sit down and explain how to do it."

"I did invoicing in my last gym, it's the same software." Even if it wasn't, it was exactly the thing I picked up in about thirty seconds flat. "I'm a computer science major too," I said lightly. Anything to relax some of the tension in the room.

He ran his fingers through his short hair. "I can't let you do anything without Nicola approving it anyway. Right now, you're only approved to coach."

"Yeah, okay." That was, or at least *sounded*, legitimate. Nicola was the boss after all. She might want to see what I could do before she gave me extra duties. After all, there was a difference between saying you could do a thing and actually being able to do it. She might have been burnt before by people not living up to their hype. It happened all the time. No doubt when she was ready, she'd take a look at what I could do and decide then.

"I guess I could tidy up out there." I nodded to some boxes and mats which were slightly out of place.

He looked relieved. "Yes, you could go and do that."

I gave him a long look but he already turned back to the screen and hunched over again. For some reason, he seemed to want me as far away from himself as he could get me.

Was Mannix really that scary standing in the door glaring at him? A little bit intimidating, sure, but not that scary. Not to me anyway. I wouldn't have thought he'd be too scary to Charlie either, but what did I know? I hardly knew the other coach.

It took me all of two or three minutes to straighten everything, before I sat on a box to eat my lunch.

I peeled open the box and frowned at the contents. I'd only packed a sandwich and a banana, but the box now contained an additional red velvet cupcake topped with black sprinkles and an edible decoration in the shape of a crown. If I had to guess, I'd think it was a collaborative effort between Ice and Mannix. I wouldn't have thought they were so romantic, but they had bought me a car. What was a little cupcake in comparison? It was sweet of them.

I was good and ate the banana first, but then couldn't resist biting into the cupcake. It was light and fluffy, and delicious. I presumed Ares hadn't contributed to it, because it didn't contain sand or gravel, or as far as I could tell, poison. Would he dare to do that, knowing the other guys might be pissed off? I liked to think, in spite of his glaring and sneering, he wasn't really an asshole. The jury was still out on that. Hopefully at some point, he would have a chance to prove me right.

I was licking crumbs off my fingers when I glanced towards the office and saw Charlie, his eyes on me. Before he realised I was looking, I saw his expression. He had the same hunger in his eyes as the guys did when they looked at me. Unlike their bold, unapologetic lust, his was laced with caution. Like he was looking at something he knew he couldn't have. But that didn't stop him from wanting it.

He realised I saw him watching and ducked down, out of sight. I was starting to think maybe he was slightly unhinged.

For the first time since we met, I felt uneasy about him. I didn't think he'd touch me or do anything to me, but working with him might be more difficult than I hoped. I wasn't going to quit. In spite of the guys' assurances they'd make all my dreams come true, I still wanted to work and make my own money. If there was anything my mother taught me, it was never to rely on other people for financial support. Especially her.

Whatever happened, I'd always want to take care of myself. I fully intended to pay the guys back for the car, even if it took me years to do it. I was going to need one hell of a good job to make enough money for that.

Soon I'd have my degree and I had a shit load of determination. I knew I had what it took to succeed. My eventual goal was to have my own company, making and maintaining security software. I had plenty of ideas brewing in the back of my mind, but I'd need a lot of money for those too. Much more than a gymnastics coach would ever make, but this was a start.

With any luck, Leo and Mum would let me keep living with them so I could save.

Who was I kidding? Mannix would insist I stay, regardless of what they said. Could he overrule his father? Probably not, but he'd try. He was at least as determined as I was. That was part of the reason I was attracted to him. In spite of his harder edge, we had some things in common. Backing down if we wanted something very much, was not an option for either of us. Not for the other two guys either, although Ice covered it by being easy-going.

Now I was thinking about the way his cock felt sliding into me, thrusting in and out. I couldn't wait to do it with him again, and with Mannix.

Okay, and with Ares. At some point, I'd need to sit down and talk to him. We needed to clear the air.

I hurried off to get a big drink of water before the next class started. There wasn't time for a cold shower, so it would have to do. I could distract myself from that line of thought by wondering again why Charlie was behaving so strangely.

That was another conversation I needed to have at some point. But not today.

CHAPTER THIRTEEN

KENNEDY

"You and my son seem to have hit it off." Leo glanced into my cup. When he found it empty, he picked it up and placed it in the dishwasher. He pulled out two clean cups from the cupboard and started the coffee machine.

"I guess you could say that," I said carefully. I made a note not to play poker against either him or Mannix. I had no idea what either of them were thinking most of the time. Leo might be making casual conversation, and he might be about to ream me out.

He glanced at me over his shoulder and raised an eyebrow. "You wouldn't say that? I got the impression you two were getting close." He turned back to the coffee machine just in time to not see my face get hot.

"Is that a problem?" I asked. Was I poking a hornet's nest with a question like that?

"That depends how many cars you need. Cappuccino?" He paused with his finger on the middle button of the coffee machine.

"Yes please, and one is extravagant enough," I said awkwardly. "I only needed an old, secondhand rust bucket."

Leo pressed the button and the machine rattled away happily. He turned around and braced his hands on the top of the island. The look he gave me was so Mannix I had to hold back a smile.

"You're going to be my stepdaughter soon. A Cassani. We have a reputation in Dusk Bay that I prefer to uphold. That means no one in the family drives around in a rust bucket." He punctuated the statement by tapping a couple of fingers on the veined, white marble.

"I wouldn't want to embarrass the family, but a Porsche?" This wasn't an argument I could win, that was obvious. In the game of pick your battles, I wasn't going to fight this one. But I could make my point. "There's plenty of cheaper cars. Are you angry he spent so much?"

"It's only money." Leo straightened up and crossed his arms over his chest.

I hadn't realised until then Mannix was very much a younger version of his father. His older brother must look like their mother. Did he have the same stubborn arrogance? Probably; it seemed to run in the family.

"If you need a replacement on a weekly basis, then it will be a problem, but in the meantime, accept the gift and enjoy it. Most twenty-one-year-olds don't drive around in cars like that."

I grinned at the understatement. "That's very true. I do appreciate it, I'm just... not used to getting gifts like that." My mother liked to be extravagant, but never like this.

"If my son has set his sights on you the way he seems to, then get used to it."

The coffee machine fell silent. He turned to pick up my coffee and handed it over to me before putting his own cup under the spout and pressing a different button.

"Thank you." I could get used to having a fancy coffee machine like this. Not to mention the quality of coffee Leo preferred. I was a tea drinker until I moved in here. I still was, but a good cappuccino helped to get me through a long day of study.

"So you don't have a problem with Mannix and I?" I asked while I waited for my drink to cool.

"Should I?" Leo picked up his black coffee and sipped. Without sugar or milk, it must have been hot, but he showed no sign of discomfort.

If anyone was uncomfortable, it was me. I shifted on my stool.

"Well, you and Mum are getting married. Some people frown on stepsiblings having a relationship with each other."

"What do you think?" He seemed genuinely curious.

"I think," I said carefully, "as long as we don't secretly find out we're biologically related, then it's not a big deal. But... if things don't work out between us, it could get ugly."

"And if things don't work out between your mother and I, the same could happen." He drank another gulp of coffee. "Things could get complicated. On the other hand, I've always thought life was too short not to take what you wanted, and worry about the consequences later."

"That sounds like something Mannix would say." I smiled.

Leo smiled back. "At the risk of being immodest, he learned from the best."

"Of course he did," I said. "It seems he learned well." In spite of being a closed book, Leo was easy to like. He was smart and respectful and obviously loved my mother.

"Where do the other two boys fit in?" Leo asked over the top of his mug.

I wasn't sure what he wanted to hear, but I decided on the truth. "Ice and I are also involved. I think he and Mannix might be involved with each other too." I watched for Leo's reaction, but he was neither surprised nor upset to hear that.

"I don't know about Ares," I added after a moment. "I think he hates me."

Leo smiled at my grimace. "I think Ares hates most people, including himself. I'm sure you'll have him eating out of your hand in no time. Did you know your mother and I started that way? When we first met, we couldn't stand each other."

I cocked my head at him. "No, I didn't know that. I thought it was love at first sight. For her anyway."

"Lust at first sight, maybe, but you don't want to hear about that. We eventually realised we had more in common than different. We're both strong person-alities."

"That's for sure," I said dryly. Once they set their sights on each other, there was no going back for either of them. I thought it was my mother who decided they should be together, but now I knew it was mutual. No one in the world could make Leo Cassani do something he didn't want to do.

"It's a trait you've inherited from your mother. That's clear to see. And one of the reasons I will allow you to be with my son. He doesn't need a weak willed woman he can walk all over. Or a weak willed man, for that matter. People like Mannix and I destroy people like that, even if we don't mean to." He seemed to be referring to someone in particular and I wondered if it was Mannix's mother. I could definitely see how guys like these would tear apart anyone without the strength to stand up to them. I wasn't sure if I was strong enough, but I'd have to be, or he'd eat me alive. Literally and figuratively.

I decided my cappuccino was cool enough to drink and took a sip. I half closed my eyes in appreciation of how delicious it was. I could do worse than a stepfather who made coffee that tasted like this.

"This is so good."

Leo grinned. "Of course it is. Nothing but the best for our family." He toasted me with his cup, then said, "Mannix says he thinks you'd be an asset to my business. Once you've finished your degree."

"I'm not really sure what you do," I admitted.

None of the guys gave me much detail, apart from Leo being powerful in some way.

"Lots of different things. I deal in transport, real estate, human resources, things like that. You could say I have my finger in several pies. Most of those pies are connected by some kind of computer network."

He smiled wryly. "You can tell by that description that I am *not* a computer person. I'd like someone close to me, someone I can trust, to be my computer person. If you're interested?"

"I'm definitely interested," I said quickly. It was an opportunity that could make me enough money to start my business the way I wanted to. When I proved myself, I might even convince him to invest. I had a feeling proving myself was going to require me to work my ass off, but that was okay. I wasn't afraid of hard work and I knew I was more than capable of doing the job.

"Of course you are," he said as though he never expected any other response from me.

What would he have said if I said no? He probably would have kept asking until I said yes, or strongly encouraged Mannix to convince me. Fortunately, that wasn't a problem.

Except for one thing.

"Shouldn't you interview a bunch of people before you decide?" Hiring me because we were more or less related, might be a rash move on his part. I didn't want anyone to think I got the job based on anything other than my skills. Hell, people would think that anyway. I'd prove them wrong.

"I know what I want and what my business needs, and that's you," he said simply. "Your mother and Mannix agreed and I trust both of them implicitly. Also, I spoke to your university and they gave me their endorsement."

My mouth formed an O. "I didn't realise you'd dug so deep."

"I always do before I approach anyone." He gave me the impression he now knew my panty size, my favourite food and that I wanted to get a tattoo of an owl on my ankle someday. Did he also know what happened that night during the ball?

No, he couldn't. He couldn't read my mind and someone like him wouldn't be involved in murder.

Right?

"I didn't mean to imply you wouldn't check out every prospective employee. I guess I just assumed..."

He raised his eyebrows at me and waited until I finished. Of course he wouldn't make it easy on me, not when he clearly expected honesty from me. He wasn't the sort of man people lied to and got away with it

I cleared my throat. "Maybe you were doing a favour for Mum. Or Mannix."

Leo put his empty cup aside and leaned his weight on his elbows. "I love your mother and my son very much, but I don't do favours like that. Not when it comes to my business. If your mother insisted I hire you, I'd still do a thorough check of you and your skills to figure out if and where you fit. And if you didn't, I'd tell her no."

I couldn't resist asking, "And if Mannix asked?"

Leo chuckled. He ducked his head for a moment, then looked back up. "Same deal. I don't trust anyone's judgement as well as I trust my own, not even my sons'. Either of them. They would be the first to bitch at me if I hired the wrong person and lost a chunk of their inheritance down the toilet."

"I'm sure they wouldn't be—" I started.

"Oh they would. They definitely would. Both of their life goals are to end up richer than me. They might even achieve it. They both have the balls for it." He looked approving.

I couldn't speak for Gunnar, but Mannix certainly had the balls and then some. Leo was right, he was ambitious. There was nothing wrong with that, so was I. I didn't necessarily aspire to be richer than Leo, especially since he was already richer than God, but I wanted to be comfortable and secure for the rest of my life. Whatever it took to achieve that. I never wanted to have to worry about money.

"I should leave you to finish your study," he said finally. "The sooner you finish, the sooner you can start to be valuable to me."

His words gave me the slightest shiver. There was nothing sexual in what he said, but for some reason, I felt like a commodity.

CHAPTER FOURTEEN

MANNIX

"Hey." I closed the door behind me and stepped over to the table.

It was covered in a variety of knives. If I hadn't met Ice, I would have assumed there were only a few different kinds of knives. You know, the ones for putting butter on bread, the kind you used to carve a chicken or some shit like that, steak knives.

There's a lot fucking more than that. Ice owns one of every single kind. Actually, that's not true. He owns a few of each. At least a dozen were spread across the table right now, each covered in a smattering of blood and other bodily stuff. I guessed it all came from the guy who hung from the ceiling in chains. He seemed to be missing most of his toes and all but his pinky fingers.

One of his kneecaps was exposed, all white and shining. The other looked to be shattered in several pieces. His face was crisscrossed with knife marks, including several across his nose.

Ice glanced over his shoulder and grinned. "Hey. You're just in time. Our friend here was just about to tell us everything he knows about Samuel Bell and his operation."

"Oh, he was? That's great." I crossed my arms over my chest and cocked my head at the man. "You might as well. He's just started with you. I've seen him keep guys alive for weeks." That was only a slight exaggeration. Ice had a knack for pushing people right to the edge, then bringing them back. He would have made one hell of a doctor, if he didn't get a bit too much enjoyment out of torturing people.

The man grunted and spat a mouthful of blood in my direction.

Ice casually walked over to the side of the room where the other end of the chain was wound around a hook in the wall. While the man whimpered, he gripped the chain and pulled, tugging the man off his feet. He dangled from the ceiling with his full weight on his damaged wrists.

I guessed it wasn't the first time he'd hoisted the man up like this.

I turned my head to the side and said, "That looks painful." Prick got no sympathy from me. He worked for the wrong side. His life choices probably didn't look so good right now. Neither did his life expectancy.

Ice grinned. "Doesn't it? It's one of my favourites. If it doesn't get them talking, it gets them thinking about talking. And if it doesn't do that, at least I can do this." He lifted up his foot and shoved it into the man's shattered knee, pushing him back before he let him go.

The man screamed as he swung back and forth, and twisted around, legs kicking and twitching.

"You get to have all the fun," I remarked.

Ice laughed. "I really do, don't I? You can join in at any time, if you like. You know what they say, the more the merrier."

He got off on this. Judging by the tent in the front of his pants, he really, really did. And that was hot as hell. I'd always had a thing for him, but seeing him here in his element made me hard too.

His gaze dipped to my groin and he took a step towards me. "It looks to me like you want to play." His hand slipped around the back of my neck and he drew me to him. He gave me a hungry kiss, stubble grazing against mine, tongue tasting my lips, before he pulled back.

"As much as I want to play some more, your father expects answers from this asshole."

I wanted to drag him over to me, push him down to his knees and make him suck my cock.

He was right though. My father expected results, and if he didn't get them soon, he'd start asking why. Worse than that, he may decide someone else would get answers quicker. We couldn't afford to fuck up so soon. Or at all. Fucking up was not an option. Not today, not ever.

Ice loosened the chain and let the man fall to the floor. He screamed as he landed on his feet, and would have crumbled to his ass if not for the chains holding him a bit too high for his comfort.

"I really don't want to keep hurting you," Ice lied. He could have kept going for days. He'd probably do it even if he didn't get paid. "Just tell us what we need to know and you can have a nice, warm shower. Maybe some coffee and pizza. Or beer. I might even patch you up and send you on your way. How about you start by telling us your name?"

"You're never going to let me live," the man growled.

"He's stubborn," Ice said. "I'm gonna call him

Stuart. Stubborn Stuart. You know what they say?"
He glanced at me, one eyebrow raised.

I decided to take the bait. "What do they say?"

"If you name something, then you have to keep
it." Ice nodded. "I don't usually bother naming the
people I work with, but I'm particularly attached to
Stuart here. I could keep playing with him for days.
He's been a ton of fun."

Luckily the building was soundproofed, and this
room was down in the basement. The whole of Dusk
Bay would have heard Stuart screaming otherwise.
Not to mention all the other people Ice worked with.

Stuart groaned. He tried to lash out at us, but it
was a weak attempt at best.

"I think he's trying to get us to kill him," I
remarked.

"You know, I think you're right."

Ice stepped closer to Stuart, almost nose to nose.
"Let's do a deal, Stuart, my friend. Tell us what we
want to know and then you can die. All of the pain
will go away. All of your broken bones and cuts and
bruises will stop hurting." He spoke in a soft, melodic
tone, like he was promising something wonderful.
Considering the state Stuart was in, it probably
would be.

I made a mental note a long time ago not to get

on the bad side of my friend here. He knew more ways to fuck people up than anyone I ever knew. Physically at least. Ares knew all the ways to get to people mentally. Me, I knew how to hit them financially. How to make their businesses crumble down around their pathetic ears. With Kennedy on board, we could attack them remotely before moving in for the kill. We'd be the perfect team of destruction and retribution. Justice, if you wanted to put it that way.

"Okay," Stuart said weakly. "I'll talk. To him." He awkwardly jerked his head in my direction.

"Ouch." Ice pouted playfully. "I thought we were getting along so well." He stepped back and gestured for me to approach.

My eyes on Stuart, I moved over to him, not quite as close as Ice got, but close enough to hear.

"Talk," I snapped.

Stuart huffed out a breath. "You're a motherfucker. Your father is a motherfucker. Your days are numbered and so are his."

I lashed out and punched him in the stomach.

He grunted, then howled in pain. The sound only lasted for a second or two before his eyes widened and he fell still.

"Mannix!" Ice drew my name out like a whine. "Did you kill Stuart? You weren't supposed to kill

Stuart." He stepped over and poked Stuart in the arm with the blade of one of his knives. The steel went right through skin and muscle and grazed against bone with a grinding sound.

"He's dead all right. That sucks. Now who am I going to play with?" He sighed, but his expression quickly returned to a smile. "Lucky for me, I can play with you and Kennedy. And Ares when he stops being a giant twat." He gave me a sideways hug and almost stabbed me in the hip with the knife.

I jumped to the side. "Watch what you're doing. I don't need you to stab me with that." The dickhead could have cut off my nuts or my cock. If he did, his would be next. I'd shove them down his throat and leave him like that for a while.

"Of course not, I have something much better to stab you with." He grabbed his groin and grinned.

My heart thudded in my chest like a hammer. I couldn't forget the way his mouth felt around my cock, and the way Kennedy watched us and got herself off. The whole thing was etched into my brain like a tattoo. Hot and hard. Both of them were beyond perfect. Them and Ares, they were the people I wanted to walk alongside on this fucked up journey, this twisted life of mine.

"As much as I'd love to, I need to report to my

father." I sighed. I didn't want anyone taking him out, but at the same time I looked forward to the day I didn't have to answer to him any more. I could just get Ice down on his knees in the fresh blood on the floor and let him blow me off. Or maybe I could let him chain Kennedy up and we could—

I shook my head. For now, I needed to focus on what I had to do, and that was tell my father about Stuart, or whatever his fucking name was.

"What are you going to tell him?" Ice asked. "The only thing I got from him was a lot of sass, and a few days of fun. Also right there, on his thigh, that's dried cum. I was having so much fun, I couldn't help myself."

I patted him on the shoulder. "You keep doing you, bro. I'll tell my dad someone is coming for us, but Stuart didn't know who it was." At least half of that was true, maybe all of it. Whatever, this was a fact he couldn't check against Stuart's word. The fact, he already knew to be true, this just confirmed it.

"Sounds reasonable," Ice said. "Maybe he can bring us someone else to play with."

I could think of at least one person I'd like to hand over to Ice and his knives. I had a conversation with Charlie, the gymnastics coach, after seeing him touch Kennedy the other day. The memory of his hands on her still made me furious, murderous.

Of course, I was nothing but pleasant to him, merely outlining exactly what would happen to him if he touched her again. I would have liked to stop him from even looking at her, or being in the same room as her, but she insisted on working at that gym, and the owner was resistant to my offers to buy the place. Charlie's sudden disappearance might freak Kennedy out, so I had to make do with a warning for now.

"I'm sure he'll find someone soon enough. If someone like the Bells are coming after us, then people like Stuart here are going to come out of the woodwork. You might need a bigger workspace. Maybe a trainee to help you with your toys."

Ice's eyes widened. "Do you think Kennedy would enjoy this? I could teach her all the things. I wonder if she likes red, too. It's my favourite colour. I like all shades of it. Especially her hair and the exact colour of fresh blood."

"You're a sick fuck, bro," I said affectionately.

He grinned. "You say the sweetest things."

"Of course I do," I agreed. "I'm a nice guy." No I wasn't, not even a little bit. I prided myself on being who I was. Hard, tough, always in control of everyone and everything around me. I was exactly the guy my father moulded me to be. The son he made in his own image, but with a harder edge, because I didn't try to be nice. Except to the three people on the face of the planet I give a shit about. For them, I would give up my soul.

Everyone else, could get fucked.

CHAPTER FIFTEEN

KENNEDY

"Night."

Working until after dark and locking up the gym with Charlie was disconcerting, until he hurried away down the street towards his car. He walked like he couldn't get away fast enough.

"Night," I said to his disappearing back. He quickly became a shadow amongst parked cars and dim streetlights. The smell of garlic hung in the air from a nearby restaurant.

I found myself alone, and shivered. Only the occasional passing car reminded me I wasn't really alone. I might as well have been as I walked to my car. My whole body was on alert, my mind replaying that night yet again.

"I could turn on my phone and find you, but

where's the fun in that? The thrill of the chase is much more entertaining. Then when I catch you, I'll know I've earned my trophy."

"There's no one here," I said under my breath. "You're overreacting because of that night." Of course I fucking was. It wasn't every day I saw a man get killed. It wasn't every night a murderer followed me through the trees. Taunted and terrified. How long would it be until I didn't freak out walking around alone at night? The fear may never leave.

Maybe past me should have been more careful, but the dark never bothered me before.

It bothered me now. A lot.

Headlights loomed behind me.

Fumbling slightly in my haste, I pressed the button on my key to unlock the car and wrenched the door open. I all but threw myself inside and slammed the door shut behind me.

The car sped past without so much as slowing.

"Stop being paranoid." I tossed my bag on the seat beside me and started the car. She purred like a big cat. I couldn't stop myself from smiling. She was an extravagant gift, but she was beautiful.

Using the Bluetooth connection with my phone, I put on the latest album from my favourite band, Wolf Venom, and pulled away from the curb.

I glanced in the rearview mirror as headlights appeared around the corner a hundred or so metres back. I didn't give them any more thought until I drove through a couple of sets of traffic lights and they were still there.

So what? I asked myself. *They're just heading in the same direction I am.*

Every so often, I'd glance up. They were no closer, but no further away either. I couldn't make out anything past the headlights, but it didn't look like a truck, and it wasn't a motorcycle. That narrowed it down to about a million other kinds of car.

I turned the stereo up for my favourite song, "Before I Stay", and sang along while trying to keep myself from what was more than likely an unnecessary freak out.

"You want to give me all of your soul,
But your eye is on the door.
Your hand is on the handle ready to turn,
But you step toward me."

I was the first to admit I had a crap singing voice, but here by myself, no one could hear me anyway, so I sang at the top of my voice. This song was so good, I couldn't help myself.

Ironic how, according to the media, the guys in

the band all shared a girlfriend, the solo singer Abbie Hart. From the sound of it, she toured the world with them and they all fell in love. How adorable was that? Not to mention inspirational. If she could handle multiple boyfriends, maybe I could too.

The song ended and I glanced up to see the car still behind me. It was a little closer now.

A shiver passed through me. I thought about calling one of the guys, or Mum, or Leo, but what would I say? *Hey, I'm driving home and a perfectly innocent car is behind me, but it's scaring me.*

Yeah, that sounded pathetic to me too.

I was only about five minutes away from home. Less if I went slightly faster. I couldn't rule out the possibility it was a police car behind me, hoping the woman in the fancy car would make a mistake and they could book me. Since that would suck, I stuck to the speed limit, but not a kilometre under.

I passed through the suburbs and into the more affluent part of Dusk Bay. Here, all the houses were enormous, and situated on several hectares of land. Most of the homes were set back from the road, so, apart from my headlights and the ones behind me, I travelled through the darkness.

I startled slightly as something darted across the road. It was just a possum, I told myself. They were everywhere around here. Them, kangaroos, and the occasional wombat. I didn't want to hit any of them, but especially the last two. They were a really good way of fucking up a perfectly good car. Not to mention I didn't want to kill any animals. All they were doing was trying to live their lives, like I was trying to live mine.

I swallowed in relief when I saw the big iron gates appear out of the darkness. I turned into the driveway and fumbled for the remote to open them.

Where the hell was it? It had to be somewhere in my bag. Please don't tell me it fell out somewhere.

I glanced out the window and saw the car was still there, but it had slowed down to almost a crawl.

Shit.

Trying as hard as I could to keep my panic at bay, I felt around in my bag until my fingers closed around the remote. Of course it was right at the bottom.

I pulled it out and aimed it at the gate before mashing the pad of my thumb against the button.

The gates never opened so slowly.

A finger.

Two fingers.

A hand.

An arm.

The car was still coming, its lights brighter now.

Just when I thought about getting out and running, the gate opened wide enough for me to gun the car and fly through.

One hand on the steering wheel, the other on the remote, I pressed the button to close the gate behind me.

In the rearview mirror and both side mirrors, I saw the car come to a stop just outside the gate. It stayed there for a minute, maybe two, then leapt forward and roared away into the darkness.

That wasn't fucking weird at all.

My heart in my throat, I drove the rest of the way up the driveway and waited again, this time for the garage door to slide open.

I slid the car in carefully and closed the door behind me. Only when I heard the clang of metal hitting concrete did I dare to kill the engine.

With my heart still racing, I reached for my bag and clutched it to my chest. I put my hand on the handle as the door opened.

I couldn't stop the shriek of fright that slipped out of my mouth.

Mannix leaned, looked into the car and grinned. His smile faded when he saw he hadn't startled me. I was genuinely scared.

"Hey," he said softly. "Didn't mean to scare you. You okay? You look like you saw a ghost."

I let him help me out of the car and close the door behind me, but it took me a moment to compose any kind of coherent words. When I finally managed to put more than one syllable together, I told him about the car.

"It was probably nothing," I said finally.

His expression was like a rock wall. Unreadable and unbreakable. "Stopping outside the gate as you come in isn't nothing. You should have called me."

"I didn't want to make a problem if there wasn't one," I argued.

"Next time, call me," he said firmly. "It doesn't matter if it's not a problem, but what if it was? What if the other car tried to drive you off the road? Or worse."

I didn't know what would be worse than being driven off the road, but his annoyance was both genuine and partly directed at me. Should I find that sweet or irritating? It wasn't my fault some dickhead followed me home.

"I should start driving you again," he said half to himself. "It wouldn't have happened then."

"You don't know that," I pointed out. "We still

might have been followed." As far as I knew, he wasn't invincible.

"You wouldn't have been alone," he growled. "If anything happened, I would have handled it." He gave me a look like he could have handled anything, including being run off the road.

"Nothing happened," I said lamely.

"This time." He pried my bag away from my chest and folded his arms around me. "I don't want anything bad to happen to you. Okay? I care about you. The idea of anyone trying to hurt you or take you away from me makes my blood boil."

He exhaled heavily out his nose. "There's a camera at the gate. I'll take a look at the footage and see if there's anything to be seen. A number plate, some distinctive features, something."

"You don't think you'll find anything, do you?" I asked softly. The headlights would have obscured most of the car, blinding the cameras to everything, including the number plate.

"Chances are, I'll see nothing but a nondescript, dark-coloured car. Whoever it was, they were probably too smart to let themselves be identified." I didn't need to see his face to know he was frustrated, his voice was full of it.

"You don't sound surprised that this happened," I said. Angry, but not surprised.

"My family... our family has our share of enemies." He leaned back to look at me. "That's one reason I worry about you being out there by yourself. Some of them wouldn't hesitate to use you to get at the rest of us."

My heart froze. "You think whoever it was, was actually after me?" Was it the three men I saw murder that man? Were they enemies of the Cassani family? Business competitors? What sort of business required murder? What the hell had I got myself into?

"It's possible," he agreed. "Or it was some kind of warning. One I can't ignore."

I looked into his eyes. "What are you going to do?" Should I tell him about that night? Maybe something I saw would be a clue to whatever happened tonight. What had I really seen though? A man killed, three men, a red and black mask. That was about it. Nothing useful. If I thought of anything, I would tell him. Until then, what was the point?

"Don't you worry about it," he said vaguely. "I'll deal with it. I'll keep you safe."

I believed him, but I was worried how far a guy like him would go to do that. He wouldn't kill anyone for me, would he? No, he probably just meant he'd go to the police and talk to them. What would they do, though?

I leaned my forehead against his chest and sighed. All I knew right now was a whole lot of nothing and that was no use to anyone. I hated feeling helpless and useless. I'd have to find a way to help keep myself safe, so I didn't have to rely on Mannix or anyone else. I was an independent woman. I could do this. I had to. Otherwise I'd never be able to sleep at night.

"I've got you." Mannix rubbed his hand up and down my back. "I won't let anyone hurt you, even if I have to keep you here at the house forever."

He meant the words to be comforting, but the fact he even thought that might be a necessity, was the most chilling thing of all.

CHAPTER SIXTEEN

KENNEDY

"You couldn't make out anything from the security camera?"

Ice looked as pissed off as Mannix had. Although, pissed for him was still a lot less intense than it was for Mannix or Ares.

Ares smirked at me like I was making something out of nothing. Ice and Mannix looked ready to pull off heads.

"Nothing," Mannix said. "Not even Kennedy arriving home. At least half an hour was completely blank."

Ares frowned. He looked more annoyed that he might be wrong than at the idea something might happen to me.

Asshole.

"That doesn't sound like a coincidence to me." Ice rubbed a hand over his jaw.

"No, it doesn't." Mannix scowled. "Kennedy, I need a list of the families whose kids do gymnastics in that last class. In fact, the whole fucking gymnasium. They'd all know when you finish. And that Charlie prick. The boss too."

I gaped at him. "I can't just give personal information out. That's all kinds of illegal."

"So is intimidation." Mannix was unmoved. "When you screw with our girl, I don't give a fuck about your privacy. All fucking bets are off. Can you get into the club's systems?"

I blinked and shook my head. "Are you suggesting I hack in?"

Ice sat forward eagerly in his chair. "Can you? I'd love to see that."

"Hacking is also illegal," I pointed out.

"Yeah, but can you do it?" Ice wasn't even slightly deterred by the illegality. If anything, he looked aroused.

"It's a simple system," I said slowly. "It wouldn't take much effort to get in, but—"

"Then do it," Mannix said. "We need to know if someone there is coming after you so we can stop them."

"Is this where you say I do something illegal or I'm going to be stuck in these four walls for the rest of my life?" I asked. I didn't like either option particularly much.

Mannix smiled. "That's exactly what I'm saying. You have access to those files when you're at work, so what's the big deal? You're just accessing them from a different place. And it's for a good cause."

I sighed. "If they have some software that tracks this back to here..." I could go to prison. I could certainly kiss my career goodbye. My degree too. This was all kinds of fucked up. Was I even considering doing this?

"We'll say Ares did it." Ice grinned.

Ares flipped him off. "Fuck off. We'll tell them she was working from home. Trying to help streamline their system. If I know anything about computers, they need it."

Nicola only just let me help with invoices, but Ares was right. The filing system the gym used was out of date and clunky, to say the least. I could easily improve it for them. I thought about offering, but I wasn't sure the excuse that I tried to do it for them from home would fly. Hopefully no one would find out what I was about to do.

I stood up, grabbed my laptop from where it lay on the island and sat back down before I opened it.

"For the record, I think this is a bad idea."

"It's a good idea if it stops anything bad from happening to you." Ice scooted over beside me, until his thigh touched mine. "In fact, I think it might be a good idea if Ares and I moved in here for a while."

To Mannix he said, "Do you think Leo will mind?"

"When I tell him why, he'll be fine with that," Mannix said. Judging by the expression on his face, he didn't much care what his father thought. If he decided they should move in, then they would.

"You wouldn't mind, would you, Beautiful?" Ice asked.

"That depends if you guys are planning to take turns following me around or some shit like that." I tapped my screen and looked for the gymnasium's website.

"That's a good idea," Ice said. "I volunteer to take all night every night." He grinned. "Don't worry, I'll let you get an hour or two of sleep here or there."

My heart skipped a beat at the idea of what he'd do to keep me awake for the rest of the time. That part didn't sound so bad.

"I don't need a bodyguard," I said.

"Guarding your body would be a bonus on top of all the other things I would do to it," Ice said.

"Could you stop thinking with your cock for two seconds?" Ares growled.

Ice shrugged. "I could, but why would I want to? Have you seen how hot this woman is? You can't tell us you don't want her as much as Mannix and I do."

Ares grunted and scowled, but he didn't deny it.

Mannix came to look over my shoulder. "Are you in yet?"

Ice grinned. "If I was in, you wouldn't have to ask."

I caught Ares' eye as we simultaneously rolled our eyes. I smiled, but he only smirked in response. Fine, if that was the way he wanted it. I wasn't going to lose any sleep over his attitude.

Mannix patted Ice on the shoulder. "Me too, bro, me too. Princess, are you in the gymnasium's files yet?"

"Almost." It was difficult to work with them talking about sex so casually. And my brain picturing where on each other they might slide into. Thinking about them fucking each other made my core hot. I needed to focus before I started to drip.

A couple of minutes later, I said, "Here we are.

The names, addresses and telephone numbers of all the students and staff, present and past."

"Can you print it out?" Mannix asked.

"Can I make a hard copy of evidence I committed a crime?" I winced. Whatever could go wrong from doing that?

"No one will ever know it came from you," he assured me. "Besides, my father and I have connections. You wouldn't get in trouble for doing something so minor."

"Is that how you get away with driving so fast?" I asked, only half joking.

He grinned. "Exactly. It helps to know people." He sounded like he meant half the city was in his pocket, but I didn't ask. If that was true, it was better I didn't know. I suspected at least some of it had to do with how rich they were. People with that much money tended to get away with a lot of shit regular people didn't.

Although, if it was true, who really were these guys?

I turned my attention back to the screen. "It should be printing out now in the study."

Leo had his own office in another part of the house, but the study was there for everyone to use. Mostly, I liked all the books in the floor to ceiling bookcases. Not that I got much time to read, but it was one of my favourite pastimes.

Mannix nodded and slipped through the door to the study. He came back a couple of minutes later with a few sheets of paper stapled together.

"This should be everything we need. I'll look through it and see who we can rule out straight away. Nova Lasalle and her family, for one. My father works f— with Daisy Lasalle and Ric DiMarco. If they wanted Kennedy dead, she'd be dead."

"I met Daze at the party you didn't want me to go to," I said slowly. "Nova is a nice kid." I frowned. "Wait a minute, what do you mean if they wanted me dead, I'd be dead?"

The guys exchanged glances. Something seemed to pass between them.

I looked from one to the other. "Is someone going to explain?"

Finally, Mannix said, "They're powerful people. Sometimes powerful people do things to get what they want. Sometimes those things are illegal."

"No shit." I nodded to the paper in his hand. "But killing people?"

Were Ric and Daze behind the murder of that man? From the way Mannix was talking, I should definitely keep my mouth shut about what I saw. If those two were that ruthless, not to mention Daze's other two boyfriends, I might end up dead. In spite of one of her boyfriends being Mannix's brother.

I rubbed the bridge of my nose. When did all of this get so complicated? And deadly?

"Desperate times call for desperate measures." Mannix shrugged. "Be glad they don't want you dead. From what I gather, Daze likes you. In this town, that's a good thing."

"You're scaring her." Ice spoke softly and put his arm around me to pull me closer. "We won't let anything happen to you, I promise." He kissed my forehead. "If anyone is going to do any killing, it will be us killing anyone who dares to lay a hand on you, or try to hurt you in any way."

"That might be a bit extreme," I said. Of course he didn't mean that literally. That would be crazy.

"Not even a little bit extreme," he said. "You belong to us and anyone who tries to mess with you, is going to learn not to."

"What he said," Mannix agreed.

Ares grunted.

"See, Ares agrees." Ice waved his hand in the direction of the other guy.

Ares looked at him like he didn't agree at all, but only grunted again.

"So what are you going to do to the people on the list you can't rule out?" I asked tentatively. All this joking about killing, if it was joking, put me on edge. If I gave all those names to the guys and they did something stupid, that would be on me. I should have refused to do it. Shouldn't I?

On the other hand, if whoever followed me tonight was on that list, and the guys could find them and hand them over to the police, then that would be a good thing, wouldn't it? I'd be that much safer.

Not just me, I quickly realised. They might do the same thing to other people. Dusk Bay might be safer without them driving around in it. Maybe there was some dubious logic in there, but it made me feel better. For now anyway.

"Don't worry about them, we'll deal with it," Mannix said. "Most of these people will be completely innocent. They have nothing to worry about. It's only the ones that aren't, that I'm concerned with. Including that Charlie prick."

"You think that was him?" I frowned. I'd considered it, but the way he disappeared so quickly...

He could have driven around the block and waited until I was leaving, to come up behind me. Why would he do that though? If he wanted to scare or intimidate me, he could do that at work. Although, he couldn't do it without me seeing him. Was he that much of a coward that he had to hide behind his car? If he was, what else might he do?

"Maybe you shouldn't go to work for a few days," Ice suggested.

"She shouldn't go at all," Mannix growled. "We can pay for everything she needs."

"I'm going to work," I said firmly. "If it's him, he's not going to try anything in front of all the kids. Or Nicola. And if it's not him, then it doesn't matter."

"I'll do everything I can to find out who it is before you have to work again." Mannix tapped the paper against his thigh. "That will solve a lot of problems. Even if Charlie wasn't the one driving that car tonight, I don't trust him. I don't like him being anywhere near you."

I sighed. "You've made that clear. He hasn't touched me again. We just work together, that's all."

"That better be all." He didn't add what he might do if it wasn't. By now I got the idea. At best, he'd make threats. At worst, he'd carry them out.

The question was, how far would he really go?

CHAPTER SEVENTEEN

MANNIX

"I have a list of potential threats." I tapped the sheet of paper against my thigh. Ice, Ares and I went over the list last night and I made a new one, leaving off anyone we ruled out. A lot of them were people known to us, or friends of ours. I underlined anyone we already knew was dubious. Some of the people on the list had a history of resentment toward those who ran this city. At least a dozen were completely unknown. I left Charlie Lynbrook on the list. His name was underlined twice.

"I'm sure my father has made you aware he believes someone is stirring up trouble."

I looked around at the faces in front of me. Daisy Lasalle, Ric DiMarco, Hamilton Blake and my brother Gunnar. Only an idiot wouldn't be alert around them. None of them, including my brother, would hesitate to kill me if it served their purpose.

I wouldn't hesitate to do the same if I had to. For now, I didn't have to. But I did have to tell them what I knew. If I didn't, and someone came after them, my life wouldn't be worth shit. And they would find out, that was guaranteed. Nothing went on in Dusk Bay they didn't know about sooner or later.

Gunnar gave me a doubtful look and put his hand out. "Let's see what you found, baby brother."

I handed him the sheet of paper, but resisted the urge to tell him to fuck off. I wasn't that much younger than him.

"Where did this list come from?" Daze asked. She regarded me with those big, dark eyes. She could almost pass for someone as sweet and naïve as Kennedy, but there was an edge to her that was sharper than any of Ice's blades. People underestimated her at their own detriment. Which was exactly how she liked it.

She was everyone's best friend, their sister, until she cut their throats. She was hot, there was no denying that, but I preferred not to have my cock burnt. Not to mention the three men in the room would take pleasure in making me suffer. I didn't want to find out how many days I'd last under their treatment.

"An associate of mine," I said carefully. "I have reason to believe they were followed by one of the people on this list, and that their intentions were to cause harm. At the very least, to intimidate. This happened right outside my home, which leads me to believe it goes further than just my associate. My father agrees it's probably something bigger than that."

I only had a brief conversation with him, but he was concerned. Not worried, but interested in having me take care of the matter before it became a major problem.

"They're getting bold," Ric said. He had an interesting array of scars on his neck. None deep, it almost looked like several people tried to cut his throat, but failed. That fit with the man I knew. If anyone would have a throat of iron, it would be him. Not to mention that if several people wanted to kill anyone, it would be Ric DiMarco. He'd pissed off his fair share of people.

"Do you have any evidence they're going after anyone but your father?" Hilton Blake fixed me with his cold blue eyes. Of all the men in the room, he intimidated me the most. He was the right-hand man of the most powerful mobster in the state, the second most powerful in the country. That made him connected and deadly. If his bosses wanted me dead, I'd be dead last week.

I understood the reason he asked that question. If this was just about my family, his bosses might cut us loose. Why bother themselves with our troubles? Being a loyal minion only got you so far. I was determined not to let him turn on us.

"We cornered Eric Parsell a couple of weeks back. He suggested the Bell family were putting out feelers into Dusk Bay." That was all we got from him before he met with an unfortunate accident involving Ares' knife and his throat. And then Ice's knife in his eyeball.

"And we're just hearing about this now because..." Daze cocked her head at me, a dangerous glint in her eye.

"I had no proof," I said, unflinching. "It was just a rumour until someone dared to follow my associate home from work."

"Associate or step sister?" Gunnar asked. Of course he would know. Dad probably told him. Or one of the staff. Whatever, I had nothing to hide.

"Step-sister-to-be and my girlfriend." I ignored

the looks of surprise. It was good to see they didn't know everything.

"You believe someone is trying to get to you through her?" Daze asked.

I nodded. "I think someone assumed she was an easy target." When I found them, I'd use them for target practice. The guys and I had a place we liked to take people once in a while. We'd release them and hunt them down. If they got away, they'd be free.

They never got away.

"I met Kennedy at that party the other day." Daze frowned. "Put the word out that she's under my protection. Anyone who touches her can deal with us." She nodded to include me in that group. It was just as well she did, because I had no intention of handing them over if I got to them first. Whoever it was, they were mine to fuck with and tear into shreds. If there was anything left when the guys and I were done, then they could have them.

"I appreciate that," I said. "She doesn't deserve to have anything bad happen to her." I was sorely tempted to insist she stay at home, focus on her degree and on me and the other guys. It would be a lot easier to keep her safe if she didn't leave.

Being the beautiful bird she was, she needed to

spread her wings and fly, even if it was only short distances. The three of us guys were now taking turns keeping an eye on her at all times. I'd spent hours this morning sitting in my car outside the gym, watching who was coming and going and making sure she was all right. She had no idea I was there, and that was okay.

Right now, Ares was reluctantly watching her while reading up on shit for his masters degree. Personally, I didn't know why he bothered to continue studying, but if he enjoyed it and it didn't get in the way, then he could do whatever the fuck he wanted. Apparently he was determined to get his PhD someday.

I supposed Doctor Ares Turner had a ring to it. Ice was taking a break, but he wanted that title too. Doctor Isaac Miller sounded fancy as fuck. Me, I was okay just being Mannix Cassani. I didn't need any fancy titles.

Although, now I thought about it, I wondered if Kennedy would do a PhD too. Fuck, I'd be surrounded by doctors. Good thing none of them would be the medical kind, not really. The medical kind were a pain in the ass. Sometimes literally.

"Are you the right person for her to be hanging out with then?" Gunnar asked. "No offence, little brother, but trouble follows you around wherever you go. If she's so nice, she might be better off nowhere near you."

I didn't bother to try to hide my irritation. It was just like him to judge my life choices.

"That's up to her," I said coldly. "If she wants to walk away, she can." It wasn't that simple. I wouldn't let her go without a fight. If she decided to leave, I'd have to convince her to stay. Or force her. Whatever it took. She was mine, no matter what.

Gunnar gave me a look like he was reading my mind, but since that was impossible and I didn't care what he thought, I ignored him.

"I can keep her safe," I said firmly, "don't worry about that. But knowing she has extra protection can't hurt." Unless it made her an even bigger target than she already is. In which case, we'd get her out of town. Out of the country if we had to.

"Of course it can't," Daze said. "Most people know not to fuck with what's mine. That includes anyone under my protection."

In the corner of my eye, I caught Ric staring at her. The front of his pants tented. Clearly I wasn't the only one who appreciated a woman who had power and knew how to use it.

If it wasn't for Kennedy, my cock would have twitched too. Neither my cock nor I would cheat, especially not on someone as gorgeous as my Princess. I'd be a fucking idiot to do that to her. I couldn't wait to fuck her. I knew she was a thousand percent worth waiting for. Sure, I was a bit pissed off Ice screwed her first, but my cock would feel her wet heat around me soon enough. Maybe tonight.

"We'll take a look at this list of yours." Hilton took it from Gunnar and skimmed his eyes down the page. "If anyone on it is up to something, we'll know soon enough." He didn't look like he believed they'd find anything.

It was an effort to keep from bristling, I reminded myself who his bosses were and forced myself to keep my face expressionless while I nodded.

"I'm sure it will be useful. When it is, I hope you'll bring us in to deal with them. Ice Miller, in particular, has a useful skill set for dealing with people who step out of line."

"I've heard that." Daze twirled a section of hair around her finger. "I'm a big fan of breaking fingers myself, but it sounds like he takes it all to a whole new level. I'll have to sit in on his work someday."

I smiled. "I think you'll like what you see." She might be just the person to introduce Kennedy to our ways. The darker, bloodier aspects of it, anyway.

Women bonding over torture and murder, what could be better?

"I'm sure I will," Daze assured me. "You boys didn't spend all that time at Brutham Academy without learning skills that will be useful to me. To all of us."

That was the point of Brutham Academy. All of the degrees were tailored not just to gain employment, but to help all the student's families in their criminal activities. Not every student came from a mobster family, but those who didn't tended to end up in the life anyway, persuaded there by their friends, and the lure of money and power. Those who refused tended not to last there very long. They either left, or they died. Either way, they got weeded out quickly.

Even those who came from mobster families got weeded out quickly if they weren't up to scratch. The level of hazing at Brutham was brutal, to say the least. It sucked when you were in first year, but by the time you got to your third or fourth and got to haze the newbies, it was worth it.

I got particular pleasure out of seeing Ice trying out some new pain inflicting techniques on the Brantley twins, Hunter and Parker. Those two were a pair of smartasses if I ever saw them. They'd do well at Brutham. Their kind always did. It didn't hurt that they were Reuben Brantley's youngest brothers. Even hazing had its limits when there was the potential of dealing with someone as powerful as him. Fuck that. Fun only went so far.

"I hope to show that my skills are, as you say, useful," I said. Useful enough that they might side-step my father in future dealings and come straight to me.

CHAPTER EIGHTEEN

"So, psychology, hmmm?" It wasn't the most exciting conversation starter, but it was a start. I was making an effort at least.

Ares barely glanced up at me and grunted. He looked back down at his laptop.

Okay then.

I took the opportunity to study him, since he was trying so hard to avoid looking at me. Or interacting with me in any way.

He wore a tight-fitting black T-shirt that moulded to his muscles like a second skin. His biceps looked like they were going to burst out of his sleeves. A tattoo of a snake slithered down his arm, ending just before his wrist. His torn black jeans were equally tight, showing off muscular thighs. Long, pale lashes lay across the top of his cheeks. What was it with guys having lashes like that? Mine were almost nonexistent.

"Like something you see?" he said without looking up. "Didn't your mother teach you it's rude to stare?"

"Didn't yours teach you to use your words and not caveman sounds?" I retorted.

"There's no such thing as cavemen," he said. "They never really existed."

"Neanderthal sounds then," I conceded. "Either way, it's not real, modern speech."

"Neither are emojis, but I bet you use them when you text your little friends." He tapped at his keyboard.

Little friends? I couldn't deny using emojis. Didn't everyone?

"Are you saying you don't use emojis?" I asked in disbelief. "I bet you do. Your favourite ones are probably the doughnut, and the hot face."

He glanced up long enough to shake his head at me, before looking back down. "Your favourite one is probably the eggplant. You don't seem to be able to get enough of Mannix and Ice's."

I'd had sex all of once in my life and he was trying to slutshame me?

"First of all, I'm pretty sure the eggplant emoji is everyone's favourite. Second of all, are you jealous because I've been spending time with them and not you? Or are you just pissed off that you're on guard duty?"

A frown flickered across his brow. "I'm just studying. Trying to anyway. When Mannix suggested I stay here, I didn't realise I'd be subjected to constant interruption."

"You're denying you're my guard today?" I asked. I wasn't fooled. Was anyone?

"Is that why you're being annoying?" he snapped. "Because you don't like the idea of being watched over? Let me tell you something." He fixed his gorgeous blue eyes on mine. "I have better things to do than babysit a spoilt brat like you." He raised the pitch of his voice and said, *"Buy me a new car. Make it as expensive as fuck and I'll spread my legs for you."*

Rather than showing him how offensive his words were, I just smiled.

"Is that what it takes to get you into bed?"

He snorted. "You fucking wish. You have the other two eating out of your hands and wrapped around your pussy. Not me. I see right through people like you."

Okay, now I let my irritation show. "People like me? What is that supposed to mean?"

"It means you saw how much money Mannix has and moved straight on in. How many days were you here before you fell on your back and spread your legs?" He looked disgusted.

"Fuck. You." I returned his look. "I don't care about his money. Or Ice's. Or yours, for that matter. In case you hadn't noticed, I'm studying so I can get a good job and make my own money. I don't need, or want, anyone else's. He didn't have to buy me a car. He sure as hell didn't need to buy me an expensive one. You might not have noticed, but Mannix is headstrong and makes up his own mind about the things he does. And people he does."

I hesitated for a moment, then added, "Are you that threatened by me?"

He barked a laugh. "Why would I be threatened by you? One little car driving behind you and you're ready to jump out of your skin." He raised his voice again. "Mannix! Ice! There's a car behind me! O! M! G!"

I stared at him. "You saw the tape. You saw the way the car stopped outside the gate. You don't think that was fucking weird? I bet anything if that happened to you, you'd wet your pants."

"Not a chance," he said immediately. "I would have put the car into reverse and smashed the shit out of the other one. Or made the asshole get the fuck out of there. Or I would have led him to one of the dozens of places in Dusk Bay where I could have gotten behind him, boxed him in and beat the shit out of him. I wouldn't have run away."

"Me trying to beat the shit out of someone wouldn't end well for me," I said. "For one thing, we don't know if there was one person in the car or five." A woman alone with five men would definitely be bad news for me. I'd take running and hiding over that any day.

He shrugged. "Next time, call for help and we'll beat the shit out of him. Or them. Or whatever."

"Are you saying you'd come to my rescue?" I asked. "Even though I'm a spoilt brat, according to you."

"Just because I don't like you doesn't mean I want anything bad to happen to you," he said. "Besides, the other guys would drag me along, whether I wanted to go or not. Now they've staked their claim on you, they're not going to let you go, no matter what it takes to keep you."

"What about you?" I found myself asking. "Are you going to try to stake your claim too?" Did I want him to? He was a massive asshole, but sitting this close to him made my body throb. I couldn't help imagining the way it would feel to have his hands on me, touching me, parting my thighs. His face diving between my legs. His cock sliding into my pussy.

His eyebrows quirked. "Flushed cheeks, dilated pupils, shallow breathing. All classic signs of arousal. You hate my guts, but you *want* me to claim you." He sat forward slightly. "If I took you over to that couch," he jerked his head to the side, "bent you over it and pulled up that skirt of yours, you'd be dripping for me. I wouldn't need to touch you, you'd be so wet, I could slide my cock right in. I could pound you so hard I'd ruin that precious little pussy of yours. And you know what you would do? You'd beg me for more."

He sat back and looked smug.

I cleared my throat and waited until my racing heart slowed. What was it with these guys and their ability to get me going with only words?

"That sounds like a yes to me," I said when I could finally speak. "You do want to stake a claim to me."

He did, I saw it on his face, but he rolled his eyes. "If I ever lose my self control and fuck you, that would be all it was. Just a fuck. If you ever think I'll have feelings for you, forget it right now. The only feelings I have toward you are annoyance, irritation and..." He paused for a moment. "No, that's about it."

"Good," I said. "Because that's exactly what I feel for you too."

"I'm glad we understand each other. I'd hate for you to be living under some delusion in which Mannix, Ice and I are some kind of harem for you. As long as you're with them, I'll tolerate you, but only for their sake."

"I'm glad we cleared that up." I picked up my empty coffee cup and slipped off my stool. "I'll do my best to stay off your cock."

"You do that," he said as though this was some kind of rational conversation we were having. "I'll do my best to stay out of your pussy."

"Good." I turned on the coffee machine. "I'm sure, between us, we can prevent any nasty accidents."

"That might be the most sensible thing I've heard you say," he said.

That was bullshit; I'd said plenty of sensible things in his presence, but I didn't dignify it with an answer. I didn't know why he decided to hate me, but he had and apparently there was nothing I could do to change his mind. I asked myself why it mattered so much, but the only answer I had was that he was Mannix and Ice's friend and it was easier if we all got along. It had absolutely nothing to do with the way my pulse raced whenever he was around. Or the way he'd come to my rescue with or without the other guys. I didn't call him out on that, but we both knew it was true. If I needed him to beat the shit out of anyone—I hoped I never did—he'd do it.

"This is where I should offer to make you a coffee —" I started.

Before I could tell him he could think again, he said, "I'd love one, thanks. Strong, like me."

I smiled sweetly. "So lots of sugar and a shit load of milk then?" That would make it as weak as coffee could be.

He snorted a laugh. "Good try, but we both know I meant super strong. And extra thick." His gaze dropped toward his groin.

"I didn't realise we were talking about the head on your shoulders," I said tartly. "Extra thick sounds exactly right."

"And yet, you're thinking about my nice, thick cock right now, aren't you?" He smirked.

Yeah, unfortunately he was right. The idea of slipping and accidentally falling on his cock didn't sound so bad right now. If only he wasn't an arrogant, self-centred, smug asshole. The fact he was made him easier to resist. Kinda.

"Are you studying psychology so you can be a therapist some day?" I asked. "Or just so you can be even more annoying by pretending to read what's going on in people's heads?"

"I don't need to pretend," he said. "Most people wear whatever they're thinking on their faces like a mask."

I knew his choice of words was coincidental, but they still sent a spike of unease up and down my spine.

I went right back to that night.

"They're going to be pissed off I let you go, but don't worry. I'll deal with them. I know just the way to handle them, like I know how to handle you. You're probably thinking I don't have a clue, but I know more than you might imagine. Such a sweet perfume, little mouse. I don't mean the stuff you dabbed on behind your ears and on your wrists. I mean the scent of you. Your pussy. Your arousal. Your fear." He took a long, slow sniff of the air. *"Intoxicating."*

Without realising, I whimpered softly.

"Holy shit," Ares whispered. "Don't do that."

I slammed right back into the present.

I swallowed and blinked, reorienting myself. I

was in the kitchen, making coffee. Not hiding in the bushes.

My eyes found his. "Don't do what?"

"Don't make sounds like that or I might forget to keep my cock out of your pussy." He made a face like he was in pain. My whimper must have turned him on hard. Any other time, I might have found it funny, but right now the memory of a black and red mask lurked in the back of my mind. It chased all thoughts of humour away.

"Right," I said distractedly. I grabbed another cup and started to make him a coffee.

Anything to keep my mind off the memory of that dark, bloody night.

CHAPTER NINETEEN

KENNEDY

My laptop slammed shut, narrowly missing squashing my fingers.

I jumped and glanced up to see Mannix, his face centimetres from mine. I hadn't even noticed he was in the room.

Yes I did, I realised after a moment. I felt the air get heavier. Thicker. He had a way of filling a space just by being in it. Owning every centimetre of it. My nipples hardened in response to his presence, even if the rest of me was focused on work. Hussies.

"Time for a break." His hand stayed pressed down on my laptop. The expression on his gorgeous face suggested he'd throw it in the pool if I refused.

I glanced at the clock on the wall. How did it get

that late? I hadn't even realised the sun set an hour ago. My stomach rumbled impatiently.

"I guess I could use a short one." I started working on this report three or four hours ago. I wasn't much closer to finishing, but I needed to eat. Maybe then I could focus better.

Every time I tried, my brain went back to that night, distracting me and making my palms sweat. Several times, I found myself scrolling through social media, just to take my thoughts of everything.

I couldn't even remember what I saw, or whose posts I liked. Everything was a blur of random videos, interspersed with a friend's photos of her poodles. Those, I remembered. Her dogs were too cute to forget. Unfortunately, cute wasn't going to get my report finished.

"Yes, you could." He was clearly not taking no for an answer. So what else was new?

"Come on." He grabbed my hand and pulled me with him through the sliding doors that led out the pool. On the grass beside it, a blanket was spread out, covered with pillows and a couple of large baskets.

"You organised a picnic?" When did he have time for that? Not to mention, how did he arrange food when I was working in the kitchen? I must have been very distracted by those poodles.

"I organised it, but one of the staff put it together. Since I can't cook, I ordered all the food in." He tugged me down to the blanket beside him and opened one of the baskets.

"I wasn't sure what you liked, so I got a bunch of stuff."

He drew out a box of spring rolls and one of fried rice. Another box contained everything we needed to put together tacos. Yet another contained pizza. The last one was full of a variety of rolls of sushi. In the other basket, was a couple of glasses and a bottle of wine.

"There's cola too if you don't like wine."

"I've never really had it." I leaned back against the pillows and tried to take in everything. "This is amazing." I was speechless that he did something so thoughtful. So... romantic. In a million years, I wouldn't have guessed he'd be into gestures like this. The unexpected sweetness made my heart flutter.

He flashed a smile. "Of course it is. You're worth it. The hardest part was getting the other guys to fuck off for a while."

"Oh." I glanced around. I wondered where they were. Neither was ever far from Mannix, especially Ice. If I had to, I'd have guessed they were lurking around somewhere, waiting for the food to be opened. Then, like a pair of vultures, they'd descend on it.

"I sent them to deal with some business-related stuff," Mannix supplied. "They'll be gone for hours." He growled like they better not hurry back, or they'd have to answer to him.

Ares might stay away, but we'd probably see Ice the minute he got back. Even if the food didn't draw him in, us being out here having a picnic would. Like the proverbial moth to flame.

"Also, my dad and Helen are having dinner in the city. They do that at least once a month."

"Right." I nodded. Mum mentioned something about that. She seemed disappointed it wasn't once a week, or every night. The woman did like her comforts. Although, since most of our meals were cooked by a Michelin starred chef, I didn't think she had too much to complain about. Honestly, I was happy eating grilled cheese or instant noodles. I was used to that at uni. The food here was a whole new level of decadence for me. One I could get used to, even if my waistline couldn't.

"I gave Francisco the night off," Mannix added.

"You thought of everything." I accepted the glass of wine he handed me and sniffed. It was soft and sweet. 'A delicate bouquet,' I thought wine people would describe it. "This smells good."

"It's a rosé. Apparently it tastes like fruit juice." He took a sip and nodded appreciatively. "Tastes like my childhood, but alcoholic."

I sipped and found he was right. I'd have to be careful. A girl could drink a lot of it without meaning to.

"What do you want to eat? I can order us something else if you don't like any of this?" He'd do it too. If I told him I wanted a triple chocolate cheesecake, he'd have one on its way in moments. That thought alone added at least three kilos to my hips.

"No, this is plenty," I said quickly. There was almost too much to choose from. "Maybe some sushi for starters? None with avocado. I'm allergic." Not deathly so, but my face would resemble a red balloon for a few hours if I ate it.

"None of it has avocado. I checked with your mother before I ordered anything." He piled a plate high with sushi rolls and handed it to me.

"I'm impressed you'd take the time to do that," I admitted. "Most people wouldn't bother."

"I'm not most people." He piled sushi onto his own plate and leaned back on his hand. "I like to do things right the first time. Besides, I made it my mission to learn everything about you. Your likes, dislikes, pet hates."

I grimaced. "Like most people, one of my biggest pet hates is the expression pet hate. I mean, it sounds so cute, but at the same time not." Was I making any sense? I hadn't had that much wine yet, had I?

He chuckled. "Yeah, it does sound kinda dumb. What else annoys you as much as that?"

I swallowed my mouthful. The sushi was so good. So fresh.

"I don't like pickles on hamburgers. Or beetroot for that matter. I don't like people who park in the middle of two parking spaces."

"Does anyone? The amount of times I've been tempted to..." He shook his head. He finished with, "It's annoying as fuck."

I'd had just enough wine to ask, "Tempted to do what? Key the side of their car?"

"More like key the side of their face," he growled. "The car did nothing wrong."

"Yeah. I guess it's not okay to take it out on the car." I wasn't sure I advocated scraping a piece of metal along someone's face either, but people do things in the heat of the moment.

He huffed out a breath. "What else? How about

things you like? Apart from me and Ice that is. And computer shit."

I wasn't sure how I felt about him referring to what I did as 'computer shit'. "I like chocolate covered liquorice. In fact, I like chocolate covered pretty much everything."

"Good to know." He looked sly. "I'm sure you'd love chocolate covered cock."

My face heated. "I might. I'm sure Ice would too."

Mannix leaned closer to me. "You want to see that, Princess? Because I can arrange it. You can have a front row seat to watch Ice suck chocolate sauce off my cock."

His words ignited my core.

"I would like to see that," I said softly. I was about to add, 'But only if you want to do it.'

I remembered what Mannix said about asking for what I wanted, and taking it, so I didn't. Of *course*, they'd only do it if they wanted to. If they did, I'd be into it.

"I'll sort it out." He brushed his lips over mine, then sat up to refill both of our glasses and drag the taco ingredients over closer.

"Let me guess, you like it stuffed as full as you can get." The look he shot me was questioning and heated at the same time.

"That's exactly how I like it," I agreed. My taco and, from my limited experience, my pussy.

"That's my girl." He put every possible ingredient into the taco except the guacamole. "Extra sour cream for you." He smiled like he was putting cum on my taco before he handed it to me.

Either way, I bit into it and closed my eyes in appreciation.

"Tacos are one of my favourite foods."

"Mine too." He leaned over to lick sour cream off the side of my mouth. "Mmm, delicious. And the dinner isn't bad either." He sat back and ate his.

"This is nice." I looked up at the stars while I ate. For a little while, I forgot about everything. Study, the stalker, murder, even Ares' antagonism.

"I spoke to your father the other day."

I didn't expect Mannix to stiffen the way he did. His response was immediate, his whole body alert, wary.

I shrank back slightly, involuntarily. Was that the wrong thing to say? If I ruined our—I guessed I could call this a date—I'd be disappointed in myself. I didn't realise his father was a hot button topic in any way.

"You did?" he asked carefully. "What about?"

"Just about us." I spoke with forced lightness. "I

got the impression you talked to him about us too. He seems to approve, as long as things don't get messy."

"Right." Mannix relaxed visibly. "I told him. Assured him things wouldn't get messy. He assured me the same thing about your mother. If *they* do, it's no big deal. We're solid, you and I."

"Are we?" I asked. "What are we, exactly? Step siblings with benefits?"

Something flashed behind his eyes, but it was gone before I could identify it.

"You're my girlfriend," he said. "And Ice's girlfriend. Someday, you'll be Ares' girlfriend too." He made it all sound so simple, so straightforward. Maybe it was that simple. Maybe I was the only one making it complicated.

"And you're my boyfriends. Isn't that a little weird? I know polyamory is nothing new, but I don't know anyone in that kind of relationship. Except the band Wolf Venom."

"There you go then. We can be as cool as they are." He finished his taco and handed me a napkin before wiping his fingers on another one.

"That's a stretch," I said, "that I could ever be as cool as them."

"I've met most of them and let me tell you, you're much cooler than they are." He said it like meeting one of the biggest rock bands in the world was no big deal.

Meanwhile, I gaped at him. "You've met them? How?"

"Daze's boyfriend Ric is the drummer, Asher's, cousin," Mannix explained. "And my father works with the brother of the lead singer, Zeke Brantley. They don't come to Dusk Bay often, but when they do, Ric always throws a party and invites everyone. I'll make sure you come the next time."

Come was the right word for it, because I was so excited at the prospect of meeting them, I might do just that. Aside from Mannix, Ice and Ares, Zeke Brantley was one of the hottest guys on the face of the planet. I might even have photos of him on my phone. And the keyboard player, Penn. And... Okay, they were all hot. Their girlfriend was a lucky woman.

"On the other hand, if you're going to look at them like that, I'm going to tie you to my bed and make sure you stay there." He looked slightly annoyed. Was he actually jealous of me fangirling over famous musicians? I wouldn't have a chance with any of them even if they were single.

"I'm not going to throw myself at them," I argued.

"You better not," he growled. "I'd hate to have to

take a hit out on a whole band just to keep them away from you."

I wasn't sure if he was joking or not.

"If you care about me, you won't kill my favourite band." Softly I added, "I know who I belong to. I just like their music, that's all."

He seemed placated by that. "They're just regular guys who happened to be famous at the moment. That's all. When their fifteen minutes of fame are over, you'll forget all about them."

I hoped they didn't stop making music anytime soon, but I didn't want to get into an argument over a rock band, of all things. No doubt he was right, they were just regular guys, and Mannix and the others were so much more than that. They were like no one else I ever met. Intense, intelligent and off the charts hot. How could any rock band compete?

"Why would I want them anyway, when I have you?" I asked.

"Exactly." He started to pack up the picnic. "Let's go for that swim we talked about. After that, I hope you're ready for me to fuck you, because I'm more than ready."

Before I could answer, he rose, scooped me up in his arms and jumped into the pool.

We were both fully dressed.

CHAPTER TWENTY

KENNEDY

I squealed, but snapped my mouth shut right before I slipped under the surface and drank a bunch of salty pool water.

Mannix let go of me when our feet touched the bottom. I paddled wildly until I shot back up and sucked in a gulp of oxygen.

"What the fuck?" I pushed wet hair off my face. My clothes clung to me, heavy as hell. I shot him a dirty look and paddled over to grab hold of the side.

Mannix bobbed up and down in the middle of the pool. He was grinning like the idiot he might just be, since he tried to drown us both.

"You were never in any danger. I'm an excellent swimmer."

"I'm not," I growled. I looked down at myself. My favourite white T-shirt, with the Wolf Venom logo on the front, was practically transparent. My drenched, black bra did nothing to hide my pebbled nipples. My shorts and panties stuck like they were glued on.

"I like you wet." He paddled over and braced himself, one hand on either side of me. "You look like a gift I need to open."

He slammed his mouth down on mine. Wet with pool water, our lips slid against each other. He pinned me to the side of the pool with his body, his full length pressed against me.

On principle, I should have pushed him away. I really wasn't much of a swimmer and drowning was not on my to-do list today. But the moment his mouth met mine, I forgot to be angry, and instead slipped my arms around his neck. My legs went around his waist, partly to get him closer and partly to keep me from sliding under the water again.

"That's my girl," he said against my mouth. He reached down and peeled my T-shirt up and over my head before tossing it onto the pool deck. At least he had the sense not to drop it into the water.

My bra went next.

His lips broke off from my mouth and he leaned

me back so he could lavish attention on my nipples with his lips and tongue.

"You're so fucking perfect."

It might have been the wine that made me bold, but I grabbed the hem of his dark grey T-shirt and helped him out of it. I tossed it aside somewhere, maybe the pool deck, and let my hands roam across his chiselled stomach and hips.

"Are you made out of stone or something?" I asked. Every bit of him was so hard, like a statue. Maybe he was a Greek god in a past life. Or some other kind of god. The gorgeous kind.

"I might be," he said, his voice muffled by my nipple. "My cock is hard for you." He unwound my arm from his neck and guided my hand down to his length.

He wasn't wrong. Even through his jeans, he was hard, hot and thick.

After a breathless moment or two, I said, "I'm ready."

Because he was Mannix, he couldn't make it that easy on me.

"Ready for what?" He rolled his hips to press his cock deeper into my hand.

"You know what." My face heated. Would I ever stop blushing at the idea of sex?

"Do I?" He grazed his teeth over my nipple and made me groan.

I managed to say, "I'm ready to be with you. To... let you fuck me."

"That wasn't so hard, was it?"

"Not as hard as you," I agreed.

He chuckled and helped me out of my shorts and panties. He placed his hands on my hips and lifted me up to the side of the pool.

Instinctively, I put my hands over my breasts.

He grabbed my wrists and pulled them away. "No hiding yourself. You're beautiful."

"What if someone sees?" For all I knew, my mother was looking out the window, exactly in our direction. Okay, I knew she and Leo wouldn't be back for hours, and all the staff would have gone home by now.

"Let them see," Mannix said. "The whole world should know how stunning you are and that you're mine. All of this—" he nodded up and down my body "—is glorious."

He let my wrists go and gripped my thighs instead. He opened my legs wide enough to place his face between them. He wasn't gentle when he attacked my clit and folds with his tongue. He was merciless, like he hadn't eaten a crumb of food.

Instead, he feasted on me. It was nothing like the first time we were together like this. He was gentle then, considerate of my virginity. Tonight, he wasn't leaving one drop on the table.

Under the onslaught, I forgot to care that I was naked. All I knew was the way his mouth felt on me, his teeth nipping my clit, tongue slipping inside me. He pushed a finger inside, then another one. He hooked his hand around to stroke me from the inside.

I arched my back, thrusting my breasts out further, lost in a world of pleasure.

"Mannix..." I said breathlessly.

He lifted his shining face up enough to say, "I like it when you say my name. Say it again." He lowered his mouth back to me.

I said his name again and again until I came, bucking and groaning against his mouth.

"I'll never get tired of that sound either." He kissed his way down the inside of my thigh to my knee and back up the other leg. "So perfect."

He placed his hands on the side of the pool and in one smooth motion pushed himself up to lie beside me. He shed his jeans and boxers as if they didn't stick hard to his body.

"Maybe we should go somewhere no one can see?" I suggested.

He grabbed my wrists again and pinned me to the hard tile beside the pool. "Let them watch. They might learn something." He nudged my legs open with his knees and knelt between them.

He lifted himself up on his arms like he was doing a push-up and said, "Look how hard I am for you, Princess. My cock is aching for you. Aching for your warm, wet, tight pussy."

He certainly looked hard. And big. His piercing shone in the light that shone up from under the water.

I swallowed hard.

He lowered himself back down until he rested on his knees and elbows, and positioned his cock outside my entrance.

"Usually, I like to fuck from behind, but I want to see your face. I want to watch you watching me fuck you. I want you to remember our first time together for the rest of your life. Let it be seared into your mind like my brand on your skin."

Without another word, he pushed straight into me. Like his tongue, he showed no mercy. He gave me no time to get used to him, not until he was balls deep inside me. Then he stilled, watching me and savouring the way I felt, and the way our bodies joined together.

He made an incoherent sound, somewhere between a gasp, a grunt and a word of some kind.

"Holy shit."

Now *that* I understood.

"You're so fucking tight, Princess. It's like the warmest, wettest vice I ever felt around my cock."

I'd probably forget to ask him how often he put a vice around his cock, but it was still a good question. I suspect he meant it all metaphorically though. Maybe.

When I finally got used to him, let my muscles relax, I savoured the way he felt, filling me so full and deep.

"You feel pretty amazing yourself," I said.

When he started to move inside me, I forgot to worry that we were right beside the pool. The only thing that mattered, was right there, right then, in the moment. His cock slid in and out of me, his piercing massaging my insides.

He hooked his arms under my legs and brought them up over his shoulders. He pulled all the way out and slammed into me so hard I felt like he might rearrange my insides. It hurt, but it same time it felt so fucking good.

I groaned.

"Mannix..."

"Princess..." He thrust harder and faster. "You're mine. This precious pussy is mine. I'm going to fuck you so hard you can't walk for a week. I'm going to shatter your sweet, amazing pussy." He drove into me so hard it bordered on viciousness, but the harder he drove, the more I wanted.

My back slid up and down the tiles made slick by the water still dripping off our bodies. If it wasn't for Mannix's weight holding me in place, I might have flown across the pool deck.

He grunted. His breath was coming in ragged pants now.

"Princess," he breathed. "Kennedy."

It was the first time I remember him saying my name. I liked the way it sounded on his lips. I liked it almost as much as his nickname for me. I wondered what Ares' nickname for me would be. Probably something along the lines of 'spoiled brat.' Or just brat for short. As if he could talk. He was more spoiled than I would ever be.

Still, thinking of him made me wonder how it would feel to have him in my mouth and Mannix in my pussy. And Ice... He could be wherever he wanted to be. I had a feeling he had some creative ideas I'd discover at some point. Hopefully at some point soon.

Mannix pulled one of my legs over his head and faced me while he went on thrusting.

"You have no idea how beautiful you are, do you?" he asked. "Inside and out. Beautiful, and you belong to me. All mine."

I watched his face in fascination while he fucked me. Every expression of concentration and pleasure. He was so gorgeous, this moment couldn't possibly be real. At any moment now, I'd wake up and find myself fucking my vibrator, lost in my own fantasy.

I hoped that *wouldn't* happen soon. This fantasy was incredible. If anyone was around, I hoped they didn't pinch me. I never wanted to come out of this.

"I belong to you," I whispered.

"You definitely do. I'm going to come inside your gorgeous body. I'm going to fill you up with my cum, so full. So fucking full. And you're going to take every single drop. That's what you were made for. You were made for me to fill you up with my cock and cum. You were born for this moment. You and your tight, wet pussy."

Between his words and his thrusts, I came again, breaking apart into a million pieces, each a drop of throbbing, lava hot blood. I threw back my head and cried out his name, even though I could barely remember my own.

"Good girl, Princess."

He rammed into me harder than ever, faster and faster until he finally stilled and groaned.

"Yes, yes, yes. Princess." He grunted. "Fuck, yes. Ahhh. Fuuuuck." He sagged, panting, his fingers digging into my hip. "You were everything I imagined and more. So much more." He nuzzled his face into my wet hair and sighed near my ear.

"So perfect."

I didn't know about that, but I didn't try to correct him. There was no point, he'd only insist he was right.

"Let's go inside and have a shower," he said after a few minutes of lying there on the tiles. "I'm going to see how many times I can make you come before you beg me to let you sleep. Just so you know, I'm going to make you come one more time after that."

"Don't threaten me with a good time." I searched around and picked up my clothes off the pool deck.

He chuckled. "Princess, you haven't even started to see a good time yet. You can still walk, can't you? When I'm done with you, you won't be able to. And that's not a threat, it's a promise."

CHAPTER TWENTY-ONE

I hung on to the silk with my thighs and one hand. Slowly, the fabric started to unwind. Faster and faster until the gym became a blur. I tipped my head back and laughed. The sensation of spinning out of control was heady, addictive. Like my whole life since I moved to Dusk Bay.

Unlike my life, I was in complete control here. To anyone watching, it looked like a wild ride, but with a snap of my wrists, a slide down the silk, I could stop it.

I didn't want to. I wanted to spin and spin forever. To fly in a blur of motion until I was too dizzy to hold on anymore. Even then, I'd cling and wish to go faster and faster.

Like always, the spinning slowed and everything

came back into sharp focus. The well used gym; boxes still scattered from the afternoon's classes; Charlie replenishing the chalk tub. Nicola was in the office for most of the day, doing admin, but she left an hour or so ago.

Reluctantly, I slipped down to the mat.

"Isn't that dangerous?"

I hadn't seen Mannix and Ice enter the gym, but they now stood near the door, arms crossed over their chests.

It was Ice who spoke, but he didn't look concerned. Unlike Mannix, who looked ready to get a ladder, climb it and snip the silks off at the ceiling.

"It's only dangerous if you don't know what you're doing," I said. "I've been doing this for a long time, and I'm careful."

"Isn't it a circus trick?" Mannix asked. "It's not real gymnastics."

"It's not a recognised apparatus," I agreed. "But it's still fun and requires hard work and skill. Do you want to try?" I was goading him. He clearly didn't want to try, but I couldn't resist. Judging silks was like judging pole dancing. Until people tried it, they didn't know how much was involved and how difficult it really was.

"I do." Ice grinned and stepped forward.

Mannix cut him a hard look. "You'll kill yourself."

That only made Ice's grin broaden. "At least I'll die having fun."

Mannix shook his head. "You're insane. Anyway, that's not what we're here for." To me he said, "I have a surprise for you."

"Hey," Ice protested. "I was in on it too."

In my peripheral vision, I saw Charlie looking wide-eyed at both guys. He noticed me watching and hurried into the office. He reminded me of a scared rabbit.

I turned my attention back to the guys, who were in the middle of a brief argument over who was and wasn't involved with whatever the hell they were talking about.

I waited until they realised I was waiting, one eyebrow raised.

"Is one of you going to explain?"

Mannix pulled a piece of paper out of his back pocket and handed it to me. "We did a little something for you."

I eyed the paper before I took it from his hand. "What did you do?" Since the last time he did something for me—aside from the picnic—I ended up with an expensive car, there was reason to be suspicious.

"Open it." He looked more smug than usual.

I gave them both a look, then slowly opened the sheet of paper.

I read it.

Read it again.

What the absolute mother-loving fuck?

"You didn't. You couldn't have."

Both of them smiled. Ice rolled from his heels to his toes and back again.

Mannix looked like the cat that got all the cream. "We could and we did. It took some time to convince Nicola to sell, but she gave in eventually."

I looked up from the deed which had my name on it. "You didn't threaten her did you?"

Mannix shrugged one shoulder. "We didn't need to. Everyone has their price and we finally reached hers. That's all."

"You didn't even want me working here and now you bought me the place? This must have cost a fortune." I couldn't get my head around it.

"It didn't cost as much as the car," Ice said. "This way, we can put in all the security measures we want to take care of you."

"What does Ares think of this?" I asked.

"He said he thinks it's idiotic, but the truth is, we'll all come here and work out. We might also have bought the building next door to put in weights and machines. Think of it as the start of your empire." Mannix spoke as if all of this was perfectly reasonable.

"All of this will help fund your dreams of having a computer security company," Ice said.

I shook my head. "You guys have put way too much thought into this. Honestly, I don't think I can accept a gift this extravagant." Especially knowing what Ares would have to say about it. Something about owing the guys a bajillion blowjobs. I hadn't even given one of them yet.

"It's in your name," Mannix said easily. "You can keep it running or shut it down. It's up to you."

"You don't want to disappoint all those kids, do you?" Ice asked. There was nothing like a bit of emotional blackmail on a Tuesday afternoon.

"Of course not, but I..." I didn't know what else to say. No one had ever done anything like this for me before.

"There is one thing," Mannix said. He strode over to the office, wrenched the door open and said, "You're fired. Get the fuck out."

Charlie turned and stared at him, wide eyed.

"Wait, no," I said quickly. "He's a good coach. The kids love him."

When Mannix turned to argue with me I said, "If this is all really mine, you'll let me hire whoever I want to hire." Nothing was ever that simple when Mannix was involved, but I couldn't let him fire Charlie because he had a problem with him. For one thing, there were laws against it. This whole enterprise wouldn't start very well if I got sued straight off.

"He might not want to stay." Mannix looked at Charlie as if daring him to contradict him.

Charlie looked at me and sat up a bit straighter. "I do want to stay. I have to eat." He looked like he was trying not to wet himself. Still, he managed to stand up to Mannix. That wasn't easy for anyone to do. He must be tougher than he looked. Or desperate.

What did I really know about him anyway? Not much. Trying to engage him in conversation was difficult. After our first meeting, he closed himself off from me.

"Then you can stay." I gave Mannix a challenging look of my own. He couldn't say I owned all of this, and then immediately override me. Well, he could, but if I let him walk all over me now, he always would. The last thing I wanted to do was throw someone out if their financial situation was so tenuous. I'd have to find time to sit down with Charlie and see if he'd open up.

"For now," Mannix said. Apparently that was all the concession he was willing to give. "But if he steps a foot out of line..." He shot Charlie a warning look.

"He won't," I said firmly. "I wouldn't be able to do any of this without him. He knows the gym a lot better than I do."

Charlie looked grateful, but at the same time very much like he wished he was anywhere but here. Or in anyone's company but Mannix.

"He looks harmless to me." Ice looked him up and down like he was assessing a piece of meat and deciding on the best way to cook him.

"I am harmless." Charlie's voice squeaked when he spoke, and his throat bobbed. "Kennedy is right, I know this gym better than anyone, including Nicola and her. I can help."

"Then it's decided. We can keep the roster as it is for now. I don't see any point changing anything, except to upgrade the computer system. I'll make that as easy a transition as I can." There was nothing worse than workplaces changing systems in such a way that staff didn't know what the fuck was going on and how to use it.

"We'll work out the security," Mannix said.

"Cameras out the front, for a start. State-of-the-art alarm system."

"This is a gym, not a bank," I pointed out.

"You're more precious than all the money in any bank," he said. "Any time you're here, I want you to be safe."

I could tell he wasn't going to back down on this, so I threw my hands up to either side and dropped them. "Fine, whatever you think we need. Just don't go spending too much money. Please."

"We make no promises," Ice said.

"None at all," Mannix agreed. "If we want to buy you things, then we're going to buy you things. What's money for if I can't use it to buy things for my princess?"

I gave Charlie a tentative smile and followed Mannix out the office door.

"What he said." Ice jerked a thumb in Mannix's direction. "Princess Beautiful deserves all the good things. If we can give it, then we will." He slipped an arm around me. "It doesn't really bother you, does it?"

"It does a bit," I admitted. "Ares said—"

"Don't worry about what Ares says. His bark is worse than his bite. Unfortunately, because a good bite is..." Ice shook his head. "It doesn't matter. The point is, we want you to have these things. And the town needs a really good gym. The other one is all the way on the other side of the city."

"And in Leo's basement," I pointed out. "He has everything you need right there."

"Everything we need," Ice agreed, "but what about the rest of Dusk Bay? We saw a hole in the market and decided to fill it. Actually, it was Mannix who saw it and made that decision."

"It's good business," Mannix said. "Wherever there's something lacking, there's a chance to make money by supplying it. In this case, making you some money. We'll help you with whatever you need, but this is your baby."

I was sure both of them, and Ares, would have a lot to say about the new gym and the old one. Mannix, in particular, liked to control everything way too much to step back from this.

"You've ordered all the equipment already haven't you?" I guessed.

Neither of them flinched or even batted an eye.

"Not all of it," Mannix said. "We need to get a builder in here to fit everything out and do the measurements before we finalise everything. We haven't even agreed on the right shade of blue to paint the inside yet."

"Maybe I don't want blue," I said.

"You don't like blue?" Mannix asked.

"I like blue, I just haven't had a chance to think about anything like that."

He slipped his arm around me. "That's what we're for. To take the stress off your shoulders."

The stress they put there.

"Maybe I should leave the setting up of that side of the business to you," I said. I might as well surrender it now, I had no hope of them stepping back from this. Did I?

"We're happy to help." Ice smiled. "What do you think about an indoor swimming pool?"

"I don't think the space is big enough." I couldn't say he wasn't ambitious. "But before you say it, this space is fine. Don't go running off finding me something bigger. Okay?"

They both looked as cagey as fuck and didn't answer.

Wonderful.

CHAPTER TWENTY-TWO

"Leo and I are thinking about bringing the wedding forward," Mum declared at dinner.

I stopped with my fork halfway to my mouth.

Mannix looked vaguely interested, but Ice and Ares didn't even pause in their eating.

I supposed it wasn't their family, not exactly. Them living here was only supposed to be temporary. No one mentioned when they were moving out again, that I knew of. They both seemed very much at home. Honestly, I was used to having them both around. I was in no hurry for them to go.

I lowered my fork. "I thought you had most of the plans made already?"

"We do, but a lot of them are flexible and those that aren't..." She turned out her hand, unconcerned.

It was only money, after all.

"Can't wait any longer huh?" Mannix asked. He glanced at me like being his step sister sooner would make our relationship spicier.

"We thought we'd waited long enough, so why wait any longer?" Mum said.

"It's only a few months," I pointed out.

"I know," she said lightly. "But look at this man. How could any woman wait any longer?" She gave him a long, loving look. It was adorable, in a sickening kind of way. I mean, she was my mother. I wanted her to be happy, but I didn't want to witness too many PDAs.

Leo, in a dark blue button down shirt with the sleeves rolled up, and a chunky watch on his wrist, looked like an older version of Mannix. The hair at his temples showed a hint of grey, and his eyes were lined in a way that suggested he smiled often. He'd be attractive if he wasn't my boyfriend's father and my mother's fiancé. If Mannix looked half as good as him at his age, we'd all be winning.

"I know I wouldn't wait," Ice said. "Life is way too short to wait for things."

"That's deep, bro," Ares said.

Ice cocked his head at him. "Isn't it? It's true though."

Something passed between them I couldn't identify. I noticed Leo watching them and had the strangest feeling he knew exactly what they were referring to. Of course, he'd known them most of their lives, so he probably had a good idea of what kind of things they got up to.

Would he tell me any of it if I asked? Then again, maybe I should wait for the guys to do that. I bet they could talk for hours about the shit they did as kids. Hell, they probably had stories they could tell about shit they did last week.

I stabbed my fork into a piece of chicken, and said, "When are you thinking of moving the wedding to?" I popped the chicken into my mouth.

"This weekend," Leo said.

I almost choked on my mouthful.

Mannix patted my back while Ares handed me a cup of water.

When I finally managed to stop coughing, I said, "That soon?" It was Monday—no wait, it was Tuesday. Tuesday night, to be specific. That only left three days to plan anything.

You know what they say, what could go wrong? At least a metric fuck ton.

"It doesn't have to be anything fancy," Mum said.

Everyone at the table snorted a laugh.

Leo chuckled. "I'm sorry, Helen, honey, but we all know we prefer fancy. I'm sure we can pull 'fancy' together in three days. Kennedy and the guys will help, won't you?"

I'd rather stick the fork in my eyeball right now, but I said, "Yeah, we will. The dresses are ready anyway." Dark green, thank fuck. Mum wanted pink, but it was Leo who suggested green would look better on everyone, including him in his waistcoat.

Common sense prevailed and Mum agreed. However, while she had made that concession, she wanted my dress and hers covered in crystals and sequins. And of course, a unique design so I could never wear it anywhere else again. Heaven forbid Mum choose something practical.

"Can we wear shorts?" Ice asked.

All eyes turned to him.

He raised his hands in surrender. "I was just asking, that's all. Shorts can be fancy."

Mum closed her eyes, and shook her head, but Leo looked amused.

"I suggested to Helen we all wear shorts or swimwear and have the ceremony beside the pool, but she didn't like the idea for some reason." He gave her a lopsided smile. The fact he genuinely loved her was clear and sweet.

I was happy for them. I wanted them both to be happy. Not just because it made life easier for everyone, but because I loved her. She was crazy at times, but she was a good person.

Mum rolled her eyes. "Like you said, we like fancy. There's nothing fancy about getting married in swimwear."

"That depends on the swimwear," Mannix said.

"And the wearer," Ice added. "I look fancy naked, and in swimwear. I'm very versatile as well as flexible."

"This is dangerously close to too much information territory," Leo said. "Maybe we can figure out how to get a cake done in time."

Ice raised his hand above his head.

"Can you bake?" I asked.

He lowered his hand and grinned. "No, but I can pile TimTams onto a plate. If you like, I can even put strawberry jam in between them." He mimed doing that with a knife.

"I'm not saying that's not fancy," Mannix said slowly.

"You're saying it's fucking nuts," Ares said. "Don't put Ice in charge of the food preparation."

"Hey, I'm really good at carving roast meat." Ice grimaced at him playfully. "But if I can't do that, I'll have to fall back on my usual role." He held both his arms up above his head and posed like a statue. "I'll be the ice sculpture."

"Ba-dum-tish," Mannix said dryly.

"Also don't let Ice think he's a work of art," Ares said. "If anyone around here is a masterpiece, it's me." He actually flexed. For real. He held up his ridiculously muscular arms and flexed. I was surprised he didn't kiss them.

Since he had muscles for days, I stared. It wasn't fair that he was so gorgeous, but such a jerk.

Ice handed me a napkin.

I turned to frown at him. "What's that for?"

"To wipe up your drool. If you stare at Ares any longer, it's going to start dribbling down your chin."

I flicked the napkin at him. "I wasn't staring."

"Yes, you were." Ares looked smug.

"Fine, I was," I said. "I was trying to understand why you think you'd be a masterpiece."

He scoffed. "You know why. You have eyes. And I have biceps as thick as my thighs."

I rolled mine. "If you say so." I turned my attention back to Mum and Leo. "I hope you're having this wedding outside, because inside isn't big enough for Ares' ego."

He flipped me off. He looked as though he

wanted to say something about one of his body parts being too big to fit inside, but he glanced at Mum and went back to eating.

Good to know he had a filter after all. Such as it was. No doubt we'd revisit this conversation later.

"The boys and I can organise our suits," Leo said. "Assuming Mannix still wants to be my best man?"

Now Mannix looked smug. "I do. It's accurate."

Ares barked a laugh, but neither Ice nor I disagreed. He was one of the two best men I knew.

"Can we call you the best Man-nix?" Ice teased.

"That's also accurate," Mannix said evenly. "So go ahead."

Ares turned to Ice and asked, "Can we call you Icehole?"

"Only if we can call you Areshead," Ice retorted. "You know, like airhead."

"We get it, Isaac," Mum said. "You boys are so funny. No wonder Kennedy likes spending time with you. You're all so sweet."

It was her turn to get stared at. There were many, many adjectives I could think of to describe the guys, but sweet?

Okay, Mannix was sweet to buy me a car and he and Ice were sweet to buy me a gym. Mannix was sweet to set up that picnic for us. Still, it didn't seem like quite the right word.

"We're funny all right," Ice said.

"Funny looking," Ares told him.

"Speak for yourself." Ice picked up his bottle of beer and took a sip.

"I'd rather speak for you." Ares tore a piece of bread off his roll and ate it. "It's much more fun."

"Don't speak with your mouth open." Ice shook a finger at him.

I frowned. "Don't you mean that he shouldn't speak with his mouth *full*?"

Ice grinned slowly. "Nope, I meant what I said. Ares shouldn't speak with his mouth open. It's much quieter around here like that."

"The only thing Ares has to say to you, I can say with one finger." Ares stuck up his middle finger at Ice.

"That was accompanied by a lot of words," Mannix pointed out. "Way more than just one skinny little finger."

"They are not skinny." Ares flipped him off with both hands.

I turned to Mum and said, "Have you thought about eloping? I hear Vegas is fun for that."

She responded with a tinkly laugh. "I'm sure

they'll behave themselves on the day. Won't you boys? I'd hate to have to insist Kennedy not have anything to do with any of you."

It was like she poured oil onto an open fire. All of the guys turned to look at her, including Leo. He seemed irritated.

Mannix's eyes were like twin chips of ice.

Ice's hand went white, he was holding his fork so tightly. He looked like he was trying to contain the urge to jump up and stab her in the forehead with it.

Ares even put a hand on Ice's shoulder like he was holding him back.

"No one will be insisting anything like that." Leo's tone matched his son's eyes. He seemed to be issuing a warning, but it wasn't to Mum. Something in his voice and posture suggested he was telling the guys to stand down.

My eyes flickered from one face to another. What the hell was going on here? I knew the guys had a slightly possessive streak—okay, very possessive streak—but they wouldn't hurt my mother if she tried to get between us. Would they? They must know if they harmed a hair on her head, I'd never speak to any of them again. She wasn't perfect, but she was my mother.

"I'm sure I won't have to," Mum said, but she

didn't back down even half a step. Was she so bad at reading the room that she didn't get how annoyed they were, or was she just not easily intimidated?

Or maybe she knew Leo would cut off Mannix's trust fund if he so much as tried to do anything to her. All hell would absolutely break loose either way.

I cleared my throat. "I thought I saw the chef making chocolate mousse for dessert."

The tension didn't evaporate, but my words broke through the mist.

"I could eat chocolate mousse," Ares said.

"We'll get ours and go and sit out near the pool," Mannix said. "I'm sure Dad and Helen have a lot to talk about." He still looked pissed as hell, but either he didn't want to be around my mother anymore or he decided to leave it to his father to deal with.

I didn't much care, as long as we got away from the air of barely contained violence.

Mannix stood. "Kennedy." He nodded at me like he expected to be obeyed.

In this mood, it was better to go along with him until he lightened up.

"I'll see you later," I said to Mum. "We can sit down tomorrow and talk about the rest of the wedding plans."

"Yes, yes." She waved us away. "Go and enjoy

yourself." It seemed she couldn't get us away from her fast enough.

Judging by the way the guys hurried into the kitchen, grabbed bowls of mousse and headed out the door, the feeling was mutual.

It was probably nothing more than pre-wedding jitters on behalf of everyone. Even the two guys not involved in the wedding. Weddings were a stressful time for everyone.

That was what I told myself, but I hadn't felt that kind of energy in the air for weeks.

Not since that night at the masked ball.

CHAPTER TWENTY-THREE

"They're a handful, those boys of yours." Mum frowned at her reflection in the mirror and went on brushing her hair.

"I don't think you could call Ares mine." I took the brush from her hand and started working on the back of her hair, running strokes slowly from the roots down to the ends.

Her hair was a couple of shades darker than mine, closer to brown than bright red.

"I've seen the way he looks at you." She smiled knowingly. "You could do worse than those three. If you can keep them in line. Leo is enough for me."

"That's good to know, because he doesn't seem like the sharing type," I said. "Except his money. He seems happy to spend that on people he cares about."

"He's very generous," Mum said. "But he's also very careful about where he invests his money. He's the kind of man who only bets on a sure thing. Like his son."

I paused my brushing for a moment. "You think my gym is a sure thing?"

"With you in charge of it, how could it not be?" she said in a way only a mother could. With faith that I'd succeed, even if that faith wasn't based on anything more than maternal love.

"Right." I swiped the brush through her hair a couple more times before I put it aside. "Do you have any idea how you want your hair for the wedding?"

In place of any kind of bachelorette party, she suggested a mother-daughter bonding evening, involving doing each other's make-up and hair and eating ice cream while watching a romcom. I interpreted that as practice for her wedding hair and make up, but it was nice to spend some time with her.

"I was thinking I could just put it up in a ponytail." She swept her hair back and looked at herself this way and that in the mirror.

I didn't know who she was trying to kid, because she wasn't kidding me. My mother wouldn't leave the house with a hairdo so simple, much less get married like that.

"How about I try a couple of things?" I suggested.

She lowered her hands and let her hair tumble to her shoulders. "You always were better at doing my hair than I was, so have at it."

I started to braid her hair from the front, drawing in pieces from the sides.

"So what does Leo invest in?" I asked.

Her body stiffened just slightly. "All sorts of things."

"Like what?" She should know that giving me a vague answer would only pique my boundless curiosity.

"Like transport and logistics. Things like that." That was only slightly less vague.

"What does he transport?" I pressed. "Ice cream? Chocolate? Dead bodies?"

I said the last without thinking, but the moment I did, memories of that night crashed back into my brain, very much unwelcome and no less terrible than they were at the time.

I was so caught up in them, I almost missed my mother's awkward laugh.

"Dead bodies? You always did have a good imagination." There was something in her tone that put me on edge.

It's my imagination, I told myself. I was jumping at shadows because I was thinking about what I saw. This might be a good chance to tell my mother about it, but something stopped me from saying the words. I couldn't put my finger on what it was, but they were stuck in my throat.

I realised I'd stopped braiding. I had to check to see which side I needed to take hair from next before I kept going.

"Someone needs to transport dead bodies," I said. "As much as they need to transport ice cream and chocolate."

"I suppose so," she said. "That looks nice, but I'm not sure that's what I want."

It took me a moment to realise she was referring to her hair.

"Oh." I stopped mid-braid and started to tease the hair loose again. "What about a bun?"

"What about curls all over?" She swept her hands through the ends of her hair and lifted them up before dropping them again. "I have a curling iron in the drawer over there." She gestured with a wave of her fingers.

Curls would take ages, but it *was* for her

wedding. I headed over to the drawer and pulled out the iron. I plugged it into the wall and waited for it to heat up.

"You never told me how you and Leo met." I held the iron near my hand and decided it was hot enough. I gripped a section of hair between my thumb and forefinger and fed it through before twisting the iron and waiting for the hair to curl around it.

"Didn't I?" She frowned at her reflection. "We met through mutual friends. More... business associates really. Reuben and Caleb Brantley. I was doing some work for them and Leo was doing some business with them. We had a few business meetings and then a few dates. The rest is history."

"Brantley? As in Zeke Brantley?" I slid the iron of her hair and let the newly formed curl bounce. Satisfied it looked good, I started on another section of hair.

"Is that their brother, the musician?" She turned her head to inspect the curl. She seemed to like what she saw.

"Musician? He's only the hottest rock star in the whole world." I rolled my eyes at myself for sounding like a fangirl.

"Good looks must run in the family then," Mum

said. "For a while there I had dreams of setting you up with one of their two youngest brothers, Hunter or Parker. They're both a couple of years younger than you though."

"Yeah, hard pass on younger guys." I wrinkled my nose. Although, if they were half as hot as Zeke, they'd be a fun package deal for some girl someday. But not for me. Not to mention two and a half guys was enough. Five might be way too much.

"There's always Joshua," Mum said. "He's a few years older than you, but he's a very successful lawyer."

"Thank you, but I have my hands full, like you said." I finished another curl and started on another.

"I'm thinking ahead, in case it doesn't work out with those boys. It's always good for a girl to have her options open."

"Do you have your options open?" I asked teasingly.

She laughed. "Of course not. I have my one and only option, but I'm not twenty-one, with my whole life in front of me. You might decide you'd prefer to look around. Sow your wild oats, whatever that means."

"I think it has something to do with farming." In

particular, ploughing, but I wasn't going to have that conversation with my mother.

"I didn't think it had to do with porridge," she said sarcastically. "Although, that's probably a euphemism for something."

"Everything is a euphemism or an innuendo if you think about it hard enough." I stepped back to inspect her hair. "How's that?" I'd only done one side so far, to see if she liked it. If she didn't, I'd try something else.

She turned her face to get a better look at my work. "That's perfect. If you can do it like that on Saturday, I might even look presentable."

"When have you ever looked anything other than presentable?" I stepped around to the other side and started to curl that.

"Never," she conceded. "But there's a first time for everything." She sighed and added, "I have to admit, I'm nervous. I know it's normal to feel that way before my wedding, I'm more jittery than usual. That was one reason I wanted to bring the wedding forward. If we waited months and months, my nerves would have gotten the better of me."

"I can't imagine anything getting the better of you, including your nerves," I said easily. Mum was the kind of person who pushed through and landed on her feet, no matter what was thrown at her, or what she went through.

"I'm good at hiding it," she said with a laugh. "Don't get me wrong, I'm excited. I can't wait to marry Leo. He's the most amazing, handsome, intelligent man I've ever met. I'm a lucky woman to have found him."

I scoffed. "He's lucky to have you. You're beautiful, smart and have the best daughter in the whole wide world." I grinned at her in the mirror.

She cocked her head, pulling against the iron slightly. "I didn't realise I had two daughters."

I laughed. "Do you really want to say that when I have a hot iron next to your head and your hair in my hand?"

"You would never hurt me," she said. "You're right, I do have the one, best daughter in the whole world. Those boys better do right by you. If they break your heart, they'll have me to deal with." Her eyes were steely. They always were when she was in full tiger mother mode. Since most of my life, it was just her and I, she had always been super protective of me. And I'd always been protective of her. Mum and Kennedy against the world. Just because Leo was in the picture now didn't mean we wouldn't look out for each other.

"If that doesn't make them shake in their boots, nothing will," I teased. I doubted those guys would be intimidated by Mum, unless Leo took her side. Things might get ugly then.

"Of course it will, I'm terrifying." She bared her teeth, but the effect was ruined when she smiled. "Okay, maybe not, but I know people who are." She looked surprised she said that out loud.

I decided a change of subject might be a good idea right about now. "I think your hair looks great like this. It's going to look perfect with your dress. Do you want my hair to look the same?" I was good at curling her hair, but I sucked hairy donkey balls at doing my own. Just like she struggled doing her own.

She looked both thoughtful and glad to be on a different topic. "I think having your hair up would suit your dress better. Don't you? I could braid your hair when you're done with mine and see how it looks. And then after that, ice cream and *Sleepless in Seattle*. Maybe some vodka."

I snapped my fingers. "I knew I forgot something." Before she looked too worried, I added, "I forgot to book the strippers." I watched the expression on her face as she went from slightly freaked out to realising I was joking.

The relief on her face was obvious.

She laughed. "Can you imagine Leo's face if strippers turned up here? Like he said, he's not into sharing. That includes me looking at half-naked men, and them grinding on me."

"Yeah, I see why he might be uncomfortable with that." The idea made my face heat. The last thing I wanted to see was some guy grinding onto my mother.

I pictured the guy's faces if they saw a stripper anywhere near me. They'd kick them straight out the door, if strippers even got in the door to start with.

Honestly, I'd feel the same way if the tables were turned. I didn't want the guys, including Ares, looking at other women dancing around and taking their clothes off. The idea gave me an irrational worm of jealousy in my stomach. It wasn't just about them looking, and maybe touching, but also about my lack of body confidence and confidence in general. I was fit enough and strong enough that my body should compete with a professional dancer, but when I looked in the mirror, I wondered what if. What if my breasts were bigger? What if I had fewer freckles? What if...

"You didn't forget the ice cream did you?" she asked.

Her words brought me back to the present.

"I'm not perfect, but I would never, ever forget the ice cream."

CHAPTER TWENTY-FOUR

"Hey." Charlie stuck his head in the office door.

I glanced over my shoulder. "Hey. I'm almost finished updating the system. Give me a couple of minutes and I'll talk you through it."

"Okay, but I have coffee." He moved so I could see his hands, a takeaway cup in each. "Kind of a thank you for not firing me. Or letting what's his name fire me."

"You should have led with coffee," I teased. "Come on in." I took the coffee he handed me and shot him a grateful smile. The one I had sitting on the desk went cold about two hours ago. The milk was probably a bunch of hardening lumps. Not even my coffee addiction could deal with that.

He leaned against the doorframe and sipped in silence for a couple of minutes. "Can I ask you something?" he asked eventually.

"That depends on what it is." I sat back and waited for the changes to update. The Internet in Dusk Bay was so fast it should be illegal. Or better yet, rolled out to the rest of Australia.

Yeah, like that would happen. Either way, the update wouldn't take long.

"What do you see in a guy like those? They both look like they want to put a collar on you and keep you on a short leash."

I tried not to bristle, because at least to some extent he was right. Mannix was a control freak who'd control every aspect of my life if I let him. Ice was... He wasn't as bad but he was protective. Ares— I suspected he might be the worst of all, if we got together. I knew from his interactions with the other guys, he'd always give me hell. But he'd bring down hell on anyone who did anything *to* me. I already felt sorry for the imaginary perpetrators.

"They like to watch out for me," I said carefully. "They care about me. It's complicated, I guess. They want the best for me."

"I want the best for you too," Charlie said. "Especially now you're my boss." He didn't seem entirely happy about that.

I sighed. "If I say I want you to just think about me as Kennedy, would you? Just because my name is on a piece of paper doesn't mean I'm not another coach. And new here too. It would be nice if we could be friends."

"That depends if your boyfriends let us be friends." He looked at me intently.

"I get to decide who I'm friends with and who I'm not," I said firmly. "I'd like to be friends with you. I don't want you thinking of me as the boss, or as someone you can't come to when you have a problem, or if you think we could be doing something differently."

After a moment I added, "Do you think there are things we can do differently?" I had a sudden mental image of him pulling a giant scroll out of his back pocket and unrolling it, before reading a list of three thousand, two hundred and twenty-four suggestions. All of which would make perfect sense, but not be free.

"There's always room for improvement," he said. "New equipment. Cappuccino machine in the staff room..."

"We don't have a staff room," I pointed out. "Oh. That's your point, isn't it? That we need a staff room?" I pinched the bridge of my nose and thought about that for a moment.

There was nowhere in the old space for it, but if we considered the space next door, maybe we could steal a few metres, even if it was shared between the gymnastics and the workout gym.

"I'll see what I can fit into the plans, but a cappuccino machine is a must." What? I wasn't exaggerating *that* much.

I sipped my coffee and made a face. It wasn't that it tasted funny, exactly, but after the coffee at home, takeaway coffee was nowhere near as tasty.

Oh good, I really was becoming spoiled.

"That bad, huh?" he asked.

"It's fine," I said quickly. To show I meant it, I gulped down the rest of it and put the empty cup on the desk. "Thank you for the coffee." Even bad coffee was better than no coffee at all.

"Any time. Especially if we really get that cappuccino machine." After Mannix almost fired him, it was awkward enough already. Strained. If I wasn't careful, that would start to impact the business and the kids. Kids, especially, were good for noticing tension, and feeding off bad energy. This place was supposed to be fun. I wanted to keep it that way.

"Okay, let me walk you through this system." I waved at the screen and moved my chair over so we could both sit in front of it. He pulled over a chair and sat. His arm brushed mine. He jumped, moving the chair away quickly before he sat back down.

He gave me a look, but didn't say anything.

I cleared my throat and started to explain, although the new system was straightforward and a lot simpler than the old one. To me anyway.

"Does that make sense?" I asked when I finished.

I realised he'd been staring at me for the last couple of minutes. Had he heard anything I said?

I turned my face to look at him. "Did I lose you?"

He blinked. "Sorry, what? Oh. No, you make perfect sense. I mean, the system. You're right, that looks a lot easier than what Nicola had set up. Quicker too. I'd much rather spend time coaching than doing paperwork."

"I'd rather be coaching, practising or drinking cappuccino than doing paperwork," I agreed. "If we do well enough, I'll hire someone to do all of this. We can focus on the things that matter. Helping make kids better gymnasts and have fun."

"I'm a big fan of both of those things," Charlie said. His expression was unreadable. He might be more like Mannix than he'd like to know, or admit. I decided against telling him that. The situation was tense enough already.

"Anyway, that's it." I turned away quickly. "The first class should be here soon."

"Right." Clearly relieved, he stood and picked up both of our empty cups to throw them in the rubbish bin.

"Just so you know, construction next door will start next week," I said before he left the office. "They know not to work while we have a class, but there's going to be some disturbance. Apparently they need to break up part of the floor and put down new concrete. After that, it shouldn't take long."

No doubt the guys would turn up at least once a day to check on the progress. And to make sure none of the tradies working next door tried anything inappropriate with me. Like smiling. Or breathing the same air.

"Great," Charlie said. "Any chance I can expand my skills by giving classes in there too? I could use the extra hours."

"I don't see why not," I said. "Let's revisit that closer to opening." I didn't even know what skills or qualifications a person needed in order to teach things like spin classes, or circuits. Or aqua aerobics, if Ice got his way. I added that to the long list of things I needed to look up or think about when I got the chance.

"Okay, boss," he said, his expression grim.

I smiled wryly. "I did sound like the boss, didn't I?" I clapped a hand to my forehead. "It's happening already." I grinned past my hand.

Charlie almost smiled before he moved away from the door to welcome the kids into the gym.

I sighed. Was the guys' buying this place a gift or a curse? On one hand, it was amazing. On the other, it was a lot of work. At least, it would be until I could hire a manager to take over the administrative stuff. All of this could very easily overwhelm me. What the hell did I know about running a business anyway?

The guys were crazy for wanting to get rid of Charlie, I decided. The only way this place was staying afloat was if I had help from someone who understood the business. He could give me a list of things needed to be changed and every single one of them would be right.

I watched through the window as he greeted the kids with a smile and a high-five.

They all grinned, clearly happy to see him. There wasn't a single one who didn't adore him. Should I make him the manager? Would he even want that? He loved what he did, but if he needed the hours, running the place would give him that.

It was another thing I would have to revisit later. I wasn't going to ask the guys for more money, so I'd have to wait until the gym was making it for me. They might try to put a collar and a short leash on me, but I wouldn't let them. I was determined to do things my way, even if I fell on my face in the process.

I caught Charlie glancing at me and looked back towards my computer screen. I hoped like hell he'd lighten up, sooner rather than later, before it made working together difficult, or even impossible.

I turned off the computer and slipped out of my chair. I should be excited. My mother was getting married tomorrow and today was the first silks class I was teaching in the gym. I finally had that report finished and only had one exam to do before my semester was done. One more semester and I could graduate.

I *should* be excited, but the nightmares persisted, even when I slept beside one or two guys every night. Even when I woke with Mannix holding me, and Ice rubbing my back. Even when we fucked until I was exhausted.

I couldn't shake the feeling they were out there and they were getting close. More than that, I felt like I was missing something. Something important.

Something in the back of my mind I didn't want to think about, or acknowledge, because the truth might be more than I could handle. Even touching it with the corner of my mind, I recoiled from it.

There was no way. I couldn't even let myself think it, not even for a nanosecond. If I thought about it, I might put together pieces I didn't want to put together.

Denial isn't just a river in Egypt. It was a wide expanse of my brain.

I wished I could erase it entirely. I wished I could go back and do that night over again. I would have stayed inside the ballroom and suffered the stifling heat, press of bodies and smell of sweat. All of that was better than this. I could have lived my life in blissful ignorance of what happened to that man that night. He still would have died, but I wouldn't have seen it. I wouldn't have known.

I shuddered.

I forced a smile onto my face and stepped out of

the office, closing the door behind me. I had to stop thinking about it, at least for a while. Focus on my class and enjoying myself.

The memory would come crashing back in soon enough.

CHAPTER TWENTY-FIVE

"This is insanity," Ares commented. He leaned against the door frame, arms crossed.

He looked good in a suit. Too good. The earthy, leather and spice smell of him flooded my senses and heated my core.

"That's one name for it." My bridesmaid dress brushed the top of my feet. The neckline plunged down between my breasts, showing off a bunch of cleavage. The back was lace, decorated with tiny green flowers.

We stood back and watched as a team of chefs and other staff prepared food for the handful of guests. Every so often, someone would run in looking for something and run back out again.

"Do you think we should help?" I asked.

"Nope," he said simply. "It's more fun to watch. Besides, if you try to help you going to trip the fuck over that dress."

I glanced down. "Yeah, you're right, I would." Before he could say anything I quickly added, "That's the one and only time I'll ever admit you're right about anything."

"No, it won't be." He smirked at me.

I rolled my eyes.

"I'm going upstairs to make sure Mum is doing okay." I carefully picked up my skirt in both hands and stepped lightly up the stairs. I didn't need to look back to know Ares watched my ass the whole way up. I didn't give him the satisfaction of glancing back to check.

I reached the top of the stairs without tripping the fuck over my dress and headed over to the room where Mum was getting ready.

Before I could knock on the door, the one on the opposite side of the wide hallway opened. Ice stuck his head out.

"Hey, Beautiful, can you do Mannix a favour and grab his bowtie? He forgot to bring it in here." He made a playful face and shrugged. "It's in the top drawer in his walk-in wardrobe. He's currently in his underwear and doesn't want your mother to see him, or he'd get it himself."

"Of course," I said before Ice disappeared and shut the door behind him. Chaos might be a better word than insanity. It seemed like Ares and I were the only ones ready.

I shook my head to myself and hurried into Mannix's room.

Like all the other rooms here, his wardrobe was enormous. Almost as big as the bedroom itself. It was stuffed full of clothes and random items, like a snowboard, which leaned against the wall. What looked like the end of a snorkel stuck out from under a pile of dirty clothes. Or were they clean clothes he hadn't put away yet? Either way, I wasn't going to start tidying up after him.

There was only one set of drawers in the wardrobe. A stack of four long ones that stretched almost from one wall to the other. Any longer and the snowboard would fit inside it. If the drawer wasn't crammed full of stuff, that was. If the floor was any indication, there wouldn't be a spare centimetre, much less a metre and a half or so.

I stepped over to the drawers and opened the top one. Just as I suspected, it was jammed full.

"In the top drawer," I muttered to myself. Ice

made it sound as though it should be easy to find. Instead, I was forced to rummage around for anything that looked like a bowtie.

I moved some superhero boxer shorts aside and froze.

A face looked back at me.

No, not a face.

A mask.

A red and black mask.

My mind skipped back to the first time I saw it.

Whatever he was going to say was cut off by the slice of the knife across his throat. He let out a gurgle. Light reflected off a gush of blood which poured from his open neck. His eyes opened wide and he sagged.

Shit.

I caught a glimpse of the mask he wore on his face. Black with splashes of red here and there. A black feather slanted from the top of either side of the mask, across his forehead. Simple, but menacing.

The denial I'd embraced so soundly, shattered. The reality came crashing into my brain. I don't know how long I'd known the truth. Maybe I'd known it all along.

The guys I'd fucked, and were falling for, and the guys I'd seen murder that man were the same people.

Hands trembling, I touched the mask. Maybe my

hand would go right through it. Maybe this was some stress induced hallucination.

My fingers bumped against plastic covered with black fabric, red fabric and feathers.

It was real.

The nightmare had found me.

THANKS FOR READING! The story continues in Prey.

If you'd like a bonus scene in Ares' point of view, you can find that here.

ABOUT THE AUTHOR

Maggie Alabaster writes reverse harem and, paranormal, sci-fi and fantasy romance.

She lives in NSW, Australia with one spouse, two daughters, one dog, and countless birds.

Jo Bradley writes contemporary romance.

Sign up for Maggie's newsletter! Sign Up!

Join Maggie's reader group! Join here!

Follow Maggie on Bookbub! Click here to follow me!

Check out Maggie's website- www.maggiealabaster.com

Sign up for Jo's newsletter

Join Jo's reader group Jo Bradley's Book Addicts

Follow Jo on Bookbub

ALSO BY MAGGIE ALABASTER

Court of Blood and Binding

Book 1 Song of Scent and Magic

Book 2 Crown of Mist and Heat

Book 3 Sword of Balm and Shadow

Book 4 Whisper of Frost and Flame

Dark Masque

Book 1 Bait

Book 2 Prey

Book 3 Trap

Saving Abbie

Book 1 Pitch

Book 2 Pound

Book 3 Session

Book 4 Muse

Book 5 Rhythm

Book 6 Encore

Novella Venomous

Saving Abbie books 1-4

Saving Abbie books 4-6 + Venomous

Ruthless Claws

Book 1 Ivory

Book 2 Crimson

Book 3 Elodie

Harmony's Magic

Book 1 Summoned by Fire

Book 2 Summoned by Fate

Book 3 Summoned by Desire

Shifter's Vault

Book 1 Discarded

Book 2 Deceived

Book 3 Disgraced

My Alien Mates

Book 1 Star Warriors

Book 2 Star Defenders

Book 3 Star Protectors

Academy of Modern Magic

Book 1 Digital Magic

Book 2 Virtual Magic

Book 3 Logical Magic

Complete Collection

Summer's Harem

Book 1: Shimmer

Book 2: Glimmer

Book 3: Flicker

Complete collection

Short reads

Taken by the Snowmen

Jingle All the Way

Also by Maggie Alabaster and Erin Yoshikawa

Caught by the Tide

Book 1–Pursued by Shadows

Book 2 Pursued by Darkness

Book 3 Pursued by Monsters

www.ingramcontent.com/pod-product-compliance
Lightning Source LLC
Chambersburg PA
CBHW020402120726
47904CB00002B/665